PENG[...]
THE RETURN OF [...]

Moni Mohsin was born and raised in Lahore, Pakistan. Married with two children, she divides her time between London and Lahore.

ALSO BY MONI MOHSIN

Tender Hooks

The End of Innocence

The Diary of a Social Butterfly

MONI MOHSIN

the Return of the Butterfly

PENGUIN BOOKS

PENGUIN BOOKS
Published by the Penguin Group
Penguin Books India Pvt. Ltd, 7th Floor, Infinity Tower C, DLF Cyber City,
Gurgaon 122 002, Haryana, India
Penguin Group (USA) Inc., 375 Hudson Street, New York, New York 10014, USA
Penguin Group (Canada), 90 Eglinton Avenue East, Suite 700,
Toronto, Ontario, M4P 2Y3, Canada (a division of Pearson Penguin Canada Inc.)
Penguin Books Ltd, 80 Strand, London WC2R 0RL, England
Penguin Ireland, 25 St Stephen's Green, Dublin 2, Ireland
(a division of Penguin Books Ltd)
Penguin Group (Australia), 707 Collins Street, Melbourne, Victoria 3008, Australia
(a division of Pearson Australia Group Pty Ltd)
Penguin Group (NZ), 67 Apollo Drive, Rosedale, Auckland 0632, New Zealand
(a division of Pearson New Zealand Ltd)
Penguin Books (South Africa) (Pty) Ltd, Block D, Rosebank Office Park,
181 Jan Smuts Avenue, Parktown North, Johannesburg 2193, South Africa

Penguin Books Ltd, Registered Offices: 80 Strand, London WC2R 0RL, England

First published in Penguin Books 2014

Copyright © Moni Mohsin 2014

ISBN 9780143423607

For sale in the Indian Subcontinent only

Typeset in Adobe Garamond Pro by Ram Das Lal, New Delhi
Printed at Thomson Press India Ltd, New Delhi

A PENGUIN RANDOM HOUSE COMPANY

For Ali, Mira, Mustafa and Abbas

Benazir's assassination leaves chasm in coming elections
Butterfly hopes Janoo will become High Commissioner in
London

There's a big fasaad in Janoo's family. And for once it's not about me. It's about the elections and whose side Janoo is taking. Basically Psycho's not talking to Janoo. (Psycho is the pet name I've given to Saiqa, Janoo's older sister. The younger one is Qubra, whom I call Cobra, pyaar say, na.) Anyways, Psycho's going round saying that qiamat is coming. Otherwise why would her own flesh and blood brother, born from same mother and same father, cut her nose and blacken her face like that by helping their second cousin to defeat her husband in the election, haan? On top, the second cousin is also from wrong side of the family, because, long ago, in fact in olden times, the second cousin's father wanted to marry Janoo's mother, The Old Bag—imagine!—and Janoo's grandfather said that no, we can't give our daughter to you because your son, he is a little bit on the demented side.

So this wrong side of the family, they've held a budge against Janoo's side of the family ever since. And in every

1

election that comes, they kharha karo a candidate of their own in Sharkpur against Janoo's brothers-in-law, who, like the show-offers that they are, are very fond of fighting elections. The wrong side of the family has never won of course, but they do it just out of saarh, to spoil the chances of Janoo's side of the family.

Janoo's got lots of votes in Sharkpur, na. Ever since he built those schools and gave all the landless pheasants sewage in their homes, he's become their favourite feudal. So Psycho thought that when her husband, Billoo, took PML-Q ka ticket he would cash in on Janoo's popularity and ride all the way to Isloo on Janoo's shoulders. PML-Q was the hot party in the last election, basically because it was Musharraf's party (even though he's a general and not supposed to have parties but still . . .). So naturally it was stuffed full of his cronies, toadies, chaprhassis and pitthoos and all. Janoo always called it the Qing's party and naturally he hated it from the bottoms of his heart because he thought that a general had no business having parties.

Anyways, because in the last election PML-Q had done so well, Billoo thought that chalo, I'll take PML-Q ka ticket again and because of my connection to Janoo I'll get all the votes in Sharkpur. And he also thought keh the evil cousin from the wrong branch of the family who took Benazir's PPP ka ticket would obviously loose. So without even bothering to ask Janoo keh bhai, is it okay with you if we use your name to win seats, Billoo and Psycho they started using his name in Sharkpur as if it was their very own while Janoo was busy being a civil society wallah in Lahore and attending this vigil and that rally and this protest and that jaloos. And even though Janoo hates PML-Q from the bottoms of his heart, he didn't go and expose Billoo in Sharkpur because he couldn't do that to his sister even though she is a shameless user.

But then Benazir bechari—hai, itna mein ne usski death ko feel kiya hai na—was killed and then Mush came on TV in an open necked shirt as if he'd just returned from playing golf and announced without even a tear in his eye or a sad look on his face that she was dead and that a lever in her Lexus jeep ki roof had hit her in the head and murdered her, and it wasn't the fundos at all and he also complied that really it was her own fault that she'd died because despite of his warnings, she'd not been security minded. And then they rushed her body out of Pindi and they washed away all the evidence the next day—I saw it with my own eyes on TV, the police hosing down the spot where she'd been killed—then tau Janoo went completely mad and decided then and there only that in Sharkpur at least her sacrifice wouldn't go in wain. So he rushed off there to go and campaign for the PPP ka candidate, who just happened to be from the wrong side of the family. But Janoo damn cared.

Since then he's being going around Sharkpur with the evil cousin and saying to his villagers that give my votes to him only and that we all owe it to Benazir. So Billoo has been deflated like a prickled balloon and Psycho's saying qiamat is coming and I'm telling Janoo that if you aren't going to stand in elections and win PPP ki seat yourself then at least let Asif Zardari know what, what you are doing for him so at least when he becomes PM he'll send you as High Remissioner to London. But will he listen? 'I'm not doing it for Asif,' he says. 'I'm doing it because it's the right thing to do. We owe Benazir and we've had enough of Musharraf. Eleven years of military rule is no joke.'

Loser jaisa. I keep telling him that we've got to get Kulchoo married off also. And just think how many nice families would want their daughters to marry him if his father became ambassador. Vaisay every time I see Mush on TV now I feel like throwing something at the screen. And if it wasn't a brand new wall-to-wall flat screen plasma, I probably would have also. Hai, mein Benazir ko itna miss karti hoon na . . .

February 2008

The nation goes to the polls
Butterfly blames Musharraf for people's bad manners

Me, Mummy and Aunty Pussy, we went to give our votes in the election. Because we are civil society types, na, who take our civil responsibilities seriously. Not like the noovo rich types who just want to stay at home and count their new cash. So anyways, I was supposed to go with Mulloo, Baby and Fluffy vaghera but they were all voting for the PML-Q kay Chaudhrys, because their husbands got big, big contracts from them in the last guvmunt but Janoo didn't, so I didn't. Go with them, I mean. Not that Janoo was interested in getting contracts—his tau shoe has more pride and self respect than to go and beg for contracts—but I still minded for him. Because I'm like that only. Loyal, principaled, tit for tit type. Anyways, I went with Aunty Pussy and Mummy because both of them were voting for PPP, na, Benazir's party.

Aunty Pussy tau has always voted for PPP. She knew Nusrat Bhutto—oho baba, Benazir's mother—from their Karachi days when both of them wore saris and beehives and meat was ten rupees a ton and only the deserving had cars and

5

even those who took their six children to school on a bicycle had happy smiles and only nice prayers for their car-driving betters. Aunty Pussy says Nusrat Bhutto always had soft spots for her and when Benazir became Prime Minister first time in the '80s, she even got Cockup Uncle, Aunty Pussy's husband, a job in some pubic sector type ki organization, where work was very little and money was very much. So I gave vote to PPP to show Mulloo vaghera that I'm not under their thumbs and Mummy gave hers to PPP because she thinks PPP is going to win and it's good to do salaam to rising sun, na.

Anyways, I told Janoo on the phone (he was in Sharkpur helping his evil relly who was fighting from PPP's side against Billoo, his brother-in-law, Psycho's husband, who was in PML-Q) that we were voting for his side only and he was very happy and then I told him why and he was not so happy. He called us the Three Disgraces. Aik tau trying to make Janoo happy is also like milking a bull.

So we went to the pooling station in our new Land Cruiser. The pooling station was in a nice sa school in our neighbourwood only. Thanks God we live in Gulberg and not some slump type area where we would have to vote alongside all the bhooka nangas. But still I was worried keh koi suicide bomber shouldn't come and blow us all up, but Mummy said, 'Don't be silly, darling, those types don't live in Gulberg.'

So many women were waiting to vote keh we had to cue. I think so lot of them were there for Benazir. Most of them looked like they were well healed types, you know silk shalwar kameezes and designer bags, but still Aunty Pussy marched straight away to the front and demanded to go first. So this woman in trainers and an oily platt, who I think so was minding the station, she asked us why. Imagine! The rudeness. So Aunty Pussy lifted her chin and said, 'Because I happen to be a personal friend of Begum Bhutto.' So this woman puts her hands on her hips, looks her up and down and says, 'I don't care if you are a personal friend of George Bush, you take your proper turn.' Imagine what the country's come to! Na koi lehaaz, na koi sharam, na koi manners. Honestly! I tell you, it's all the fault of that Musharraf. You know all that prosperity he gave to small type people, na, it went straight to their heads. So served him right when his PML-Q party and his darling Chaudhrys lost so badly, so badly that don't even ask. I tau tell you, whole gardens were flowering in my heart when I heard that PPP had won hands down. I was so glad for Benazir, so glad for Janoo and so glad for myself—now I could crow to Mulloo.

So yesterday I called up Mulloo and said, 'So sorry about the Chaudhrys. You all must be so sad, na, their loosing the election so badly.'

'Chaudhrys who, baba? I don't know who you could possibly mean,' replied Mulloo. 'We tau all voted for Nawaz Bhai and his PML-N. He's always been *such* a close friend. And I am such an admirer of his wife, Bhabi Kulsum. So upright, so religious, she's such a respiration for women. In fact, I'm just off to give mubariks with a trunk full of mithai. Byeeee.'

March 2008

Asif Zardari and Nawaz Sharif agree to form coalition government
Butterfly discovers Janoo's favourite colour

Between you, me and the four walls, Janoo, poor thing, has not been same since Benazir's murder. He's started smoking again, na. After fifteen years. Socho zara! Also has started saying strangest, crackest things. Like yesterday he told me he wanted a green car. In all the years that I've been married to him he never once told me that green was his favourite colour. Imagine! All these years he's been hiding it from me. And there I was thinking keh he liked mud brown and mouse grey. Now I find that secret, secret mein he's been fancying green all this time. I hope so he likes forest green or olive green and not parrot green or sub say worst, vomit green. I told him I'm always ready for a new car but does it have to be green? Can't it be metallic blue instead? Or a smart sa steal grey colour? With coffee coloured leather ki seats?

He sighed and said, 'Never mind.'

'So shall we get a Prado or a new Land Cruiser or even a Lexus? Tell na,' I asked, excited at the prospectus of driving into Mulloo's drive away in my gleaming si, new si, huge si silver grey car with coffee brown leather seats. (They had to sell their red Porch last year, na, because Tony got into some trouble with the banks and now Mulloo who used to swan around like a real show-offer in the Porch has to sit with a bowed head in their five year old Corolla. Serves her right, vaisay. Got her just deserts.)

And then Kulchoo, that spoilt spot, said, 'But Aba, it is actually not green to keep changing your car all the time. That's needless consumerism. The best thing you can do for the environment is to keep your old car. Just use it less.'

Use it less? If I used my car any less it would be garlanded in cobwebs. Next he'll be suggesting that I go to the bazaar myself on a bicycle every day and do the sauda. Honestly! Father tau was already crack, now son is also following in his footsteps. It's all to do with hereditary and jeans, I'm told. Aside from your looks shooks you also inherit your personality straights in your jeans. Chalo, yeh acchha hai, I thought to myself. Some people inherit lands, some inherit Swiss bank accounts, others inherit kothis, others inherit factories and firms and political parties and some inherit thick hair or green eyes or sharp cheek bones and fair si skin and what does my son inherit from his father? A cracked head. And knock knees, that's what. It's just not fair.

April 2008

Cracks appear in PPP–PML coalition
Butterfly plans a stylish funeral

I said to Janoo, 'Haw, Janoo, look what's happening!'

'What?' he said. 'Where?'

'Everywhere,' I said. 'So much of fasaad. So much of khoon kharaba. And you tau said that Zardari and Nawaz had everything in control and were doing everything nicely. Look at the collision government they've made . . .'

'It's coalition, not collision.'

'Khair whatever. But you've got to admit that the whole thing is already falling apart, no?'

'I won't hear one word against democracy!' he snapped.

Aik tau Janoo's also become so sensitive. Can't talk to him about his precious collision, can't talk to him about buying a new high power generator, can't talk to him about buying a new steal grey car with coffee coloured leather ki seats.

Chalo, goli maaro to politics but generator is a must. Abhi tak tau it's been okay with the old generator which runs just three ACs but I'm tau damned if I sit through May and June without six splits running together. Janoo can do whatever he wants. Sell his ancestral lands in Sharkpur for all I care. Janoo can try and do all the kanjoosi that he wants, naya generator tau mein lay kar rahoon gi.

Talking of kanjoosi, Mummy's family is also the limit. You know, na, that Shocky Mamu—oho bhai, Uncle Shaukat, Aunty Pussy's older brother—he had been ill for the longest time. Well, now he's not ill any more. Now he's dead. He passed out yesterday. So when Mummy called and told me I said to her that we must get Aunty Pussy to put pressure on his widow, Aunty Sheela, to give him an acchha sa, classy sa send-off. After all he gave her fifty-four years of loyal service, even more than her Singer ki sewing machine which she got in her jahez.

So I said to Mummy we must give theka for his funeral to a hot sa happening sa event manager. Get him to fly in some proper flowers, tulips from Amsterdam or Rottendam. Or else, orchids from Singapore or Bangcock. Send out black boarder waalay cards, with raised si golden lettering and black silk lined envelopes announcing his death and inviting people to the funeral. Also we have to give proper food, you know, rockets and cherry tomatoes ka salad and chicken teriyaki and prawn tempura and chocolate kay chhotay chhotay say petty fours. I hope so Aunty Sheela is not thinking of bore aloo gosht and pulao, followed by kheer. That's tau just so over. And instead of those same old white chaddars on the ground on which you have to sit across legged so you get cramps in your legs and your bottom goes to sleep, maybe we could rent delicate si rot iron ki chairs with nice say cushions in grey and black raw silk. I suppose colour scheme will have to be black but maybe with touches of ivory white and pearl grey. And all the servants should wear black uniforms that day and instead of calling maulvis to the house to read the Holy Koran maybe they could just do tape recordings on i-Pods and distribute those among the guests.

Anyways, I was going on and on like this but Mummy was silent and finally after half an hour when I stopped to take breath, she said, 'You must be mad. Sheela and Pussy would rather get their nails yanked out with rusted pliers than spend more than the absolute minimum. It's aloo gosht and saag and tiny announcement in the papers and voh bhi, sub say sasti waali akhbaar for poor old Shocky.'

'They're going to shame us all,' I wailed. 'Dunya kya kahe gi?'

'They damn care about dunya. Dunya kehti rahe jo kehti hai.'

'But Mummy, how am I going to hold my head up high among my kitty crowd if they do such a cheap sa funeral?'

'I don't know why you're getting so upset, beta,' she said. 'All your life you've known that they're like this only.'

'You're right,' I sighed. 'I suppose I'll just have to wait for your turn before I can throw a really fab funeral.'

At that Mummy slammed the phone. Aik tau Mummy's also become so touching. Just like Janoo.

May 2008

Asif Zardari reluctant to reinstate judges
Butterfly thinks of a new film for Aamir Khan

The other day, my sweepress, Jannat, she came to my room and asked me if she could have chhutti of five days to nurse her husband who has gone and got his ribs and nose and arm broken in some drunken fight on the streets. I told her that 'Why are you such a fool, haan? All he's ever done to you is beat you and take your money and do your insults and you want to nurse him? Are you crack?' So she sighed and she said, 'Bibi ji, what to do? When a dhol is slung around your neck what can you do but to drum it?' I gave her the chhutti because I like Jannat.

Once after a late night party when I got home I wrapped my diamond ear studs in a tissue paper and left them on my dressing table and next morning thinking it was just an empty tissue I threw it in the waste paper basket. Jannat found my studs and without even my asking, she returned them to me. Also she is chup chaap and respectful and Christian and I know the other servants are not nice to her because of that but she never complains.

So I gave her the chhutti but afterwards I was thinking of what she said. If a dhol is slung around your neck, what can you do but drum it? So if Jannat can look after her husband who beats her and does insults of her and takes all her money then I can also take interest in everything that interests Janoo who doesn't beat me and doesn't do my insults and doesn't take my money. So I've decided from now on, because Janoo has craze about politics, I am also going to take so much of interest, so much of interest keh poocho hi na.

So Janoo is on tender hooks. About what? About all this political uncertainty, baba, aur kya? You know, na, that he thinks that the political future of this country rests on his shoulders only. Just between you, me and the four walls, talk of being denuded! Every day from morning to night he's going on and on like a struck record about this judges ki restoration ka tamasha. Mush had got rid of the judges, na, and Asif had said he'd bring them back once he got majority and now he's got majority but he's dragging his heels and Nawaz is getting all impatient and saying to Asif that cheater, you broke your promise and the lawyers are all taking out jalooses and saying keh give us our judges back just now only. So I'm listening like a good wife to Janoo and saying, 'Haan Janoo, bilkull Janoo, sub theek Janoo.'

Janoo says all this would be a Restoration Comedy if it wasn't so tragic. He says everybody's playing politics and everybody's got their own angels and meanwhile poor lawyers are getting sun stroke in the heat from coming out in demonstrations every other day.

Apparently inside game is this: Nawaz wants to get rid of

Musharraf who is obviously still President because despite of elections, his Presidential term doesn't finish till August. So until then Mush is going to be our gullay ka haar. So Nawaz is thinking if he can bring back the Chief Justess, Iftikhar Chaudhry, who Mush threw out, then as soon as Chief Justess is back he will do tit for tit and he will immediately throw Musharraf out. Then Nawaz will urge the Chief Justess to get rid off the PPP government so that he, Nawaz, can become King of Pakistan again. But what's wrong with that, Janoo? I asked. I think so Nawaz has seen after his time in Saudi Arab that being king is sub say best. Na koi elections, na koi referendrums, na koi Parliaments, na koi motions. Bus just you and you only.

Honestly, vaisay what's the big fuss for? Mein tau kehti hoon, let the judges be restored. After all, Lahore Fort looked so nice after it was restored. And so did Jehangir's moratorium, I mean—honestly, this heat has made my brain melt also— mausoleum. So nice and fresh and clean looking after all that painting and fixing shixing. Just think how nice the Chief Justess will look after a nice sa hair cut and a bit of Botox and a nice sa make-over with a nice si wardrope and maybe a little bit of surgery to fix that squint in his eye also. I mean make-over kar hi rahe hain tau might as well go the hole hop, no? I think so he will give hundred, hundred prayers to all of us. And all his other judges also, who can also come out of their bore black suits and wear some nice si colourful si T-shirts and designer jeans with Convert type trainers. And maybe they can also varnish their beloved legal bench which they keep going on about and paint it a nice shade of 7 Up green like our flag.

Vaisay I don't think so Asif Zardari should have broken his promise but uske liye itna mein feel karti hoon na keh koi hisaab hi nahin—suddenly a single parent to three children. So maybe we should cut him some slacks.

But chalo, let's talk of something nice instead. Hai, I saw *Taare Zameen Par* for fourth time last night. Aamir Khan makes such touchy films, na, itni moving keh poocho hi na. It's about that little boy who can't read, write and spell. He's got dyspepsia, na. I think so you get it if you drink too much of Pepsi. But in my time at the Convent, if you had dyspepsia, the nuns just hit your hands with rulers and made you stand in a corner and told you you were stuppid. Like they did to Fluffy. But I think so she was tau in real life also stuppid. And I think so that dyspepsia must be contagious because everybody in the Presidency and Parliament has it also. They all claim to have BA ki degrees but I swear hardly any of them can read or write. Ub dyspepsia nahin hai tau aur kya hai? Maybe Aamir Khan can make a film about them called *Saaray Zameen Par*.

Face-off between Musharraf and lawyers intensifies
Butterfly fed up with paying bills

Hai, I'm so poor, so poor keh poocho hi na. I don't even have enough to spend on a two carrot diamond anymore. That's how poor I am. Why? Oho baba, because I'm spending every single penny that Janoo gives me on chalaaoing my kothi. Rs 1500 a day I spend on running my generator only. Cross my heart and hope to die, it's no extrageration. I said to Janoo, chalo, let's go to London or Paris or somewhere cool for summers. He said I must be joking. With the pound at Rs 135 and the dollar at 70, and fuel sir charges on all air tickets, he couldn't afford to leave the house. I said to him, at Rs 20,000 a day (if you put in atta, paani, lamb ka gosht, petrol, gas, servants' celeries and extra virgin olive oil, avocadoes and scented candles) we can't afford to stay in the house either. Not that anyone else seems to be having any trouble vaisay. Baby, Fluffy, Flopsy vaghera are tau partying away like never before. GTs and khaanas and huge, huge shaadis and all every night. Only we are losers. We and the poors.

July 2008

Militants continue recruiting youth in Swat
Butterfly deals with Mummy's phone issues

Bombs are bursting, atta is finishing, bijli is going, rivers are drying, Talibans are coming and Mummy is worrying about her phone. She called today to say that she'd had enough and she was immigrating.

'Why?' I asked, thinking maybe she'd had another phudda with Aunty Pussy.

'Bus,' she said. 'Because I'm fed up.'

'But where are you going?' I've told you, na, that Mummy's gone a bit sterile. I think so she's forgotten that like the rest of us she's a green passport holder and to immigrate somewhere your passport has to be 'billoo or mehroon', as Janoo's cousins would say. Otherwise tau you can forget about going anywhere abroad except Afghanistan and . . . um . . . Afghanistan.

'Have you had a fight with Aunty Pussy?'

'Why should I have a fight with Pussy?' she snapped. 'Are you calling me a fighter cock?'

'Haw, Mummy, just asking. You don't have to be so touching, you know.'

Aik tau everyone around me is taking offence at the drop
of a cat. Zara sa kuch keh do and they go up in smokes. I swear
it's only me left who is still normal and nice. Me and maybe
Jonkers. Otherwise tau everyone has become abnormal.

Anyways, I finally got to the bottoms of Mummy's sad
dastaan. For the last fifteen years Mummy's had this phone
wallah who works in the Gulberg exchange and makes sure
that Mummy's phone is never kharaab and her bill is never
big (I think so he sends on half her bill to her neighbours,
who live in a big house and have a joint family system so
they're always fighting with each other about who is ringing
up such a big bill and they've even had a divorce in the family
because they suspected that one of the young daughters-in-
law must be having a boyfriend in Karachi who she is calling
on the sly all the time, otherwise why they have such a big bill,
haan? Or else Mummy's line man sends her bill to her other
mean, kanjoos neighbours who refuse to use him.) Anyways,
Mummy's phone wallah comes around four times a year, at
Eids, New Years and beginnings of summers to collect his,
you know, little present.

And Mummy, as you know, is very dependent on her land
line. I've given her two, two, three, three mobile phones but
she's forever loosing her phone, leaving it in the bazaar or in
restaurants or her friend's houses and also when she has it
and it rings during her Indian TV serial kay time she puts
it on silent and then forgets to turn it on again and so you
keep calling her, keep calling her and she never picks it up
and then she says she doesn't want a mobile because no one
ever calls her on it. Also she doesn't know how to do S&M,

I mean, sorry, sorry, SMS and refuses to learn even. Tau long and short of it is, that she can't use a mobile and so her land line is basically her life line.

Anyways, Mummy had grown very fond of her phone wallah because he was such a shareef, quiet, honest type. Always spoke to her feet, never to her face, always called her 'Huzoor', always did jhuk jhuk ke salaam and whenever the present wasn't big enough, never complained, just stood there quietly in the drive away till Mummy added more and more notes till he was finally satisfied and then he left as quietly and as politely as he had come. Anyways, to cut a short story even shorter, he went and died last year.

Now new man who's inherited old man's customers is different. He calls Mummy 'Anti', as if, God forbid, he was related to us. Not Begum Sahiba, not Bibi Ji and certainly not Huzoor but 'Anti'. I think so he means 'Aunty'. On top he barges into her sitting room and stands on her carpet *without even removing his shoes*. He looks her in the face, and uss say bhi worst, he scratches, you know, over *there* the whole time. And yesterday he told her: 'Anti, itni mehngai ho gayee hai, ub hisaab kay paisay do. Varna yeh kaam naheen chalay ga. Sumjhay?'

That's why Mummy's immigrating. She says this is no longer a place where honest, decent types can live anymore.

I told her, 'Mummy, don't mind, haan, but with your passport you have only two choices: either you can go to Afghanistan or else, Upstairs to Him.'

After a while she said, 'In that case, beta, I think I'll go

Upstairs. At least I know a tameezdar, decent phone wallah there.'

'But Mummy,' I said, 'you won't need your phone there . . .'

'Kyoon ji?' she said, 'I'm sure my old phone wallah will be able to place a long distance call if I ask him nicely. After all, even Allah Mian needs to communicate occasionally . . .'

August 2008

Government tightens fiscal control over public spending
Butterfly buys a Birkin

Guess what? We are in London. So much of fun I am having jiss ka koi hisaab hi nahin. Of course first thing I did on landing was to go straight away to Selfridges and Harrods and Harry Nichols. Bought six pears of shoes from Jimmy Choo and Loubootin and four bags—one black D&G ka, one blue Prada ka, one red quilted Channel waala and one brown Gucci ka. And between you, me and the four walls, don't tell Janoo, one Birkin also. But chhota waala. After all what would the difference be between me and all those newly rich fleshy types if I also went and bought a huge Birkin? After all, as Janoo says, size matters, no?

Then I bought an arm full of make up, but only top ke brands: Shu Hamara, Channel, Calvin Clean, Landcomb vaghera. Then I got three pears of sunglasses, a suitcase full of La Perla kay underwears and four cashmere ki cardigans from Brora and two pears of nice jeans with rhino stones on the back pockets, a few designer tops to go with them—nothing much, just one Stella McCartney, one DVF, one Helmand

Lang and two Armani—and haan, almost bhool hi gayee, one dinner service for twelve, Wedgewood ki, golden and white to go with my new golden and white dining room ke curtains. And dabaa ke mein ne facials karai, had streaks put in my hairs and permanent false lashes glued on. I have to look London returned when I go back, no? All fresh, fresh, dewy, dewy.

One of Janoo's old college friends who's a gora took us to dinner at Nobu, which was very nice except for the food (all raw, raw, cold, cold). He asked me what I thought of Mr Zardari.

'I think so I would like him more without a moustache,' I replied.

'And Mr Musharraf?' he asked.

'Who's he?' I respond karoed.

I met up with Poppy and Mouse and Kamila and Sher Afzal and Meliha and Sikander and Snooky and Yawar who were all here from Lahore and Karachi and Isloo but have gone now. And I've done lots of culture also. Saw *Mama Mia*, *Kung Fu Panda* and *Sex and the City*. Kulchoo said he wanted to see something called *The Dark Knight* but I said it reminded me too much of load shedding.

Village council executes eighty-year-old man in public
Butterfly prepares for a month of fasting

Chalo, we're back in Lahore and holy month of Ramzan is here. I was tau totally ready. Went and bought nice, nice cheeses and namkeen biskutts from Agha's in Karachi for my iftaris and pineapple kay juice kay tins (hundred per cent organic) without which I can't do sehri, na. Have also got new generator, so I can sleep all day araam say baba, after keeping my roza. I think so the rest will do me goods. Itna hectic time guzra hai na just before Ramzan.

Bhai, first tau we were in London. Then we came back and had to rush off to that wedding in Karachi. Which wedding? Haw, where are you? The Tareen–Majeed wedding, baba, to which whole world had been invited. Such a zabardast wedding, yaar. Went on and on—like lawyers ki movement. Two gaanas, one by local singer and one by Indian one and then of course mehndi, shaadi and valima vaghera. Shaadi par tau so many people were there that as soon as you got inside the hall, you immediately got stuck up. I even had to call Mummy and Aunty Pussy on my mobile and ask where they were. They'd managed to find seats in some corner and they said that they daren't give them up because then someone else might take and they'd have to then stand all evening and that tau their corns wouldn't allow, na, and because I couldn't find Mummy and Aunty Pussy and their chairs in the hujoom so we never even met. Everybody was hoping that Asif Zardari would come for valima—he's best friends with Annu and Nazli Majeed, na—but I think so he was too busy peaching Mush in Parliament that day to adventure out of Isloo.

Talking of Asif Zardari, Presidential election is coming up. Mush is going, thanks God, and lots of people are standing their candidates in his place. So I am also going to kharha karo my own candidate for President. And that's Jonkers. Bhai, why not? If everyone can kharha karo their own candidate then why not me also? And anyways, what's wrong with my cousin Jonkers, haan? He's not corrupt, he has no prison record, he has a real BA degree and voh bhi foreign ki, he is not dyspeptic, has done no deals with any dictator and speaks such nice English. And also he won't take sides because the only party he's ever been in is his own birthday party. Janoo said I'd taken leaf off my senses. I said I can also say hundred, hundred things back about his senses but I won't because it's Holy Month of Ramzan and like guvmunt and Talibans I am also going to do a peace deal for this month only. But as soon as we see Eid ka moon—bhai, on chand raat only—it will be back to open warfare as usuals.

September 2008

Bombing at hotel in Islamabad kills at least forty
Janoo embarrasses Butterfly

I swear Janoo's going to make me total social outpast who nobody's going to invite again. By now you must be knowing that he's never been the life and sole of the party. Khair, that tau I'd become used to. After all, not everyone is gay like me. But now tau uss ko zabaan lag gayee hai and he's become so rude, so rude, keh I can't even tell you.

On Sunday we went to Mulloo's for iftaar party. Small si thi, just us, them, Flopsy and Dodo, VD and MT. Anyways, after iftaar we were sitting doing idhar udhar ki gup shup in their TV lounge, (they call it their 'media room', just because they have 56 inch ki screen, cheapsters) when Dodo said to Tony, 'Yaar TV laga. Khabrein dekhain.'

So Tony flicks the remote control and suddenly a flaming Marriott appears on the screen. Ussi waqt sub shock mein chalay gaye.

'Hai Allah!' howled Mulloo. 'Don't tell me it's the Marriot in Isloo. That lovely Nadia's Café where all the politicos hatch plots, and Muddy's place where we met all of Isloo's in-crowd and Dynasty Restaurant where I had that big bash for my birthday before last. All up in smoke! Ub hamara kya ho ga? Where will we hang out in Isloo now? Boo-hoo-hoo.'

'This is what comes of being America's pitthoo!' Tony shouted. 'This is what we get for hunting our fellow Muslims and fighting America's war on terror for them. Aur karein Amreeka ki khidmat! Aur banain Amreeka kay ghulam!'

'Bilkull, yaar, we're completely beghairat!' said VD.

'If you ask me,' said Flopsy, 'Musharraf must've had it done. Everyone knows he's sulking.'

I looked at Janoo. After all these years of marriage I've developed a sick sense about him. His eyes had narrowed to slips, his mouth was all tight and his forehead scrunched up like a used tissue. I jumped up and said, 'Janoo? Chalein ghar?'

'Sit down!' he growled. 'What did you mean by that comment, Tony?'

'Yaar, if you're going to give me your bloody anti-Taliban line then you can just shut up now only!'

'So what do we do? Sit back and let the Taliban go on a rampage? Annexing Pakistani territory, burning down schools, executing civilians, assassinating our leaders, rewriting our laws? We should just sit back and watch? Is that what you want?' By this time Janoo was shouting at the tops of his voice. 'Fellow Muslims indeed. Let me tell you, my friend, they don't think of you as a Muslim at all. They think you are a westernized kaffir. And you'll know it when they come to burn down YOUR vulgar little media room, and beat

27

up YOUR daughter for wearing jeans and YOUR wife for wearing lipstick and YOU for being clean-shaven. THEN you tell me! Whether you leave them alone or not, they have plans for you. And if you're not prepared to fight them, then get ready to be buggered good and proper.'

'Don't call me your friend, you beghairat CIA agent!' shouted Tony.

'Just because some people can't afford media rooms, no need to rubbish ours,' sniffed Mulloo.

'Home, Janoo? I shrieked, dragging him out of the room.

October 2008

Pakistan may seek IMF credit facility
Butterfly rushes to her bank

Mummy called me at the track of dawn today.

'Get up,' she shrieked over the phone. 'Get up at once and go to your bank and open your locker.'

'Uff Allah, Mummy!' I mumbled. 'What time is it?'

'It's late. Later than you think. Probably too late already. Get up before you loose everything.'

'Oho Mummy, what you are talking about?'

'Don't you "oho Mummy" me! They are going to seal our lockers. They're going to take our dollars and our pounds and our youros and all our gold and diamonds also. While you are lying snoring in your bed they are going to rob you black and blue.'

'Snoring? *Me* snoring? How you can tell such fat, fat lies, Mummy? You know I don't snore. *You* snore. No offence, okay, but you tau snore like a hippo, Mummy.'

'How dare you call me a hippo? Is this why I had you? And that also by Sea Section after a twenty-hour labour? Is this why I raised you? Sent you to top ka school and college

29

like the Convent and Kinnaird College? Married you off with such a fat dowry? So that in my old age you could call me a hippo? Haan? And that also when I take the trouble to call you up to warn you so that you don't get robbed? Just look at you. You don't even have itna sa gratitude. You should be ashamed of yourself.'

'Okay, tell na. Who's going to rob me?'

'Say sorry first.'

'Acchha baba, sorry, sorry. I take it all back. About you being a hippo, I mean. Or at least snoring like one. Okay? Now tell na, who's going to rob me?'

'Jee,' whispered Mummy.

'Who's Jee, for God's sake?'

'Guvmunt,' she muttered.

'Jee for guvmunt?' I asked. 'Why should guvmunt want to get inside my locker?'

'Shush, don't speak so loudly. You know they bugger our phone lines. If they know you've taken your dollars out of your bank and taken them home then they may also follow you home and rob you in your sitting room.'

'But why?'

'Oho baba! Which world you are living in? Don't you know guvmunt doesn't even have enough foreign exchange to pay the sweepers on the roads? They are bangrupt. They're up to their ears in depth and can't pay their lones. Don't you know even this much?'

'But Mummy, since when have our road sweepers been paid in dollars?'

'Tomorrow when rupee will be going to 500 for one dollar,

then even sweepers will refuse your rupees. Then guvmunt will have no choice but to pay them in dollars.'

'Haw hai! So they are going to steal my dollars from me to pay the sweepers? Don't mind, Mummy, okay, but I think so you've gone totally cracked.'

'Fine! As your mother it was my duty to tell you. Now I've told you. Bus. Don't come crying to me later when they've robbed you of all your dollars shollars and say that I didn't warn you,' she said and slammed the phone.

Aik tau Mummy has also become totally polaroid in her old age. So sensitive. So highly stung. Always harbouring suspensions about others wanting to loot her and rob her blind. I swear, she's even started locking up her sugar in case the servants steal it. But what if she's right? What if Finance Minister is already inside my locker and is trying on my gold necklaces and my bracelets even as I lie in my bed? Better call Mulloo and check if she's heard anything.

'Hello, haan, Tony Bhai? All well, thanks, by grace of Almighty Allah. Is Mulloo up? She's gone out already? Where? Would you be knowing? She's gone to her bank? Why's she gone to the bank? Just like that? Hmm. Okay thanks, Tony Bhai, got to go na, something urgent has come up. No, no, nothing serious. Just someone's trying on my necklaces and my yearrings and I've got to get them off.'

November 2008

'This is your victory': Obama
Butterfly deprived of sleep

Such a spitting headache I've got, na. Have taken three, three pana dolls and not a dot of difference they've made. Why have I got a headache? Oho baba, because all night Janoo has been keeping our bedroom waala TV on at top ka volume and watching Americans ki election. And shouting and screaming and crying himself historical.

'America has elected Barrack Hussein Obama. *Hussein?* Do you realize how huge that is? How absolutely huge?'

What's so huge about being called Hussein, haan? I wanted to ask. Mummy's driver is also called Hussein. And he's not huge from anywhere. He's tau bearly five foot tall and thin as a razor blade seen sideways.

'Mind na karna, Janoo,' I said to him, 'but zara aap over nahin ho rahe?'

'You don't understand,' he said. 'This is a historic moment. It's a victory for every underdog, for everyone who's ever struggled against the odds, for everyone who's ever had a dream. Imagine! The Americans have chosen a black man for their President. How wonderful is that? And it's barely fifty years since the Civil Rights Movement. A black man whose middle name is Hussein. A man with Muslim antecedents. Can't you see how big this is? What a dream this is? Remember Martin Luther King's prophetic words, "I have a dream . . ." Oh my God! This is better than any dream.'

Dil dil mein I said, I would also like to dream, but for that I have to be allowed to sleep, no? And how I'm going to sleep with TV playing on my head and you screaming in my year? Honestly! So selfish Janoo is, only ever thinking about himself and his own needs.

Chalo, thanks God Obama has become Prime Minister of America. Janoo tau had announced that if Obama looses then he's migrating to Mars. Humph! As if the Mars wallahs are going to give him, a Pakistani with a green passport, a visa! So unrealistic he is. So denuded. Anyways, I've tau been bored frigid watching all this erection coverage. Now I can even do an exam on Obama, so much I know about him. I know his dadehaal is in Uganda or Rwanda or some place like that in Africa and, poor things, they look so ghareeb and live in huts that look like Mulloo's servants' quarters. And everyone is going on and on about his wife, Mitchell, and how stylish she is and how impressive vaghera.

Mind na karna, par mujhay tau she didn't impress even this much. You know, so big and arms like a mazdoor's who lifts fifty, fifty bricks in one go. I tau liked that size zero Cindy Mac Cane, bhai, with her shiny golden hair and her big, big, shiny diamonds. I even liked that other one, with the glasses and the thousand children, what's her name, that mouse hunter yaar, haan Saira Paling. She was the one from Baked Alaska, no? From where she can say hello hi to Russia every day. Nice mascara, nice neat sa hair-do, nice designer clothes. But, uff baba, soooo many children. Just like our poors who have hundred, hundred children each.

Janoo's saying that Obama is going to have a tough job because he has to wind up two wars, one in Iraq and one in Afghanistan, and also at the same time economic slum has come on whole world. Apparently the economic slum is also called Credit Crunch which, between you, me and the four walls, I thought was a peanut ki toffee but it turns out is something more horrible tasting. Chalo, let Obama and Janoo chew on it . . .

November 2008

Extremists bomb Performing Arts Festival in Lahore
Butterfly not impressed by Obama

Yesterday I sacrificed two bakras and distributed the meat among the poors to say thank you to Allah Mian for saving Kulchoo's life. Ji haan, he was at the Puppet Festival yesterday where the bloody beardo weirdos let off those bombs. Kulchoo says one minute he was standing outside the performance hall with his friends eating chaat and everyone was laughing and chatting and enjoying and next minute they hear a noise like a bijli ka transformer bursting and then suddenly everyone's running and screaming and shouting 'bomb, bomb'. And there's smoke everywhere and smell of burning. Thanks God, Kulchoo and his friends had the presents of mind not to run around trying to be heroes and saving others or trying to find out what happened. They just straight away dropped their plates and sprinted out together and headed for the car park and jumped in to Kay's car and drove off.

Thanks God, bombs were small this time, but what if someone had died? Haan? Then what? And, why bomb a puppets ka show at the Performing Arts ka Festival? Because you don't like it? Array bhai, if you don't like to see puppets ka tamasha, then sit at home araam say and do knitting shitting or whatever else you enjoy. No?

Vaisay isn't it a bit iconic that these damn fool bombers who are biggest puppets of you-know-who in the tribal areas, are bombing puppets? They tau should love all puppets, and do embrace with them as their long lost brothers. For the first time ever I agree with Janoo. These bombers are holding the whole country, all hundred and eighty millions of us, to handsome.

But Janoo says just you wait, Obama will fix everyone and everything. Well, I've been waiting and seeing for a whole month now and Obama hasn't fixed anyone, not even Bush who is still sitting in White House as if it was his own baap ka ghar. I tau think, between you and me and the four walls, that Obama is a bit of a kaam chor, like our driver, Miskeen, who won't clean the sitting room windows because he says it's not his job. Vaisay have to say his wife, Mitchell (oho baba, Obama's, not Miskeen's), has started wearing some nice clothes and some nice false lashes. And I hear Saira Paling has become laughing stop in US because she says Africa is a country. Vaisay typical of Americans to think that they are the only country in the world. Bhai, why can't Africa be a country if it wants, haan?

December 2008

Taliban seize control of Swat
Butterfly gets a cold sore

Just my luck! It had to happen bang in the middle of the shaadi season. I've got this big cold store on my lip and it looks just like a collegiate implant gone wrong. One look in the mirror in the morning and I jumped back shrieking, 'Naheen, naheen! This can't be happening to me!' Everyone became very alarming and Janoo came rushing into my dressing room. When he saw me pointing to the half of my upper lip that's swollen like a tennis ball, he chuckled and said, 'What's that? A flying saucer landed on your face?'

'What cheeks!' I shrieked. And then to add result to injury, he said, 'Lip, not cheek, sweetheart. Chalo, at least you look like half an Angelina Jolie!'

So I said to him, I said, 'At least me looking like half an Angelina Jolly is better than you who looks from nowhere like George Clooney!' Then I slammed the door and locked it from inside and put on that weepy John Lemon song, 'Imagine there's no heaven' and sat in front of the dressing table looking at my swollen lip and feeling all broken and sad inside. Then I dried my tears, squared my shoulders, opened the French windows and stepped out into the miniature land-escaped garden next to my dressing room.

I sat there thinking that it's all my own fault that I get taken for granted by Janoo, his Ugly Sisters, The Old Bag, Mummy, Aunty Pussy, Jonkers, the servants and even Kulchoo. I've got such a self-defecating sense of humour, I'm too generous for my own good and I've got too much patients specially with The Gruesome Twosome who are dunya ki sub say worst sisters-in-law. I revolved there and then, sitting in my land-escaped garden, that I'm going to turn over a new leave. I said a thank you dua to Almighty Allah from the bottoms of my heart that I've come to this seclusion sooner rather than later. And as for Janoo, I decided that I should ignore him, no matter what he says, because he's been having a nervous brake out since his Danish joint-venture partners pulled out of his dairy project in Sharkpur after we (oho baba, not we as in me and Janoo but we as in us Pakistanis) went and bombed the Danish embassy in Isloo. I swear I think so I should get a medal the size of a frying pan for putting up with Janoo. No, Mummy says, you should get the Noble Prize for Peace like that Shirin Mahal woman lawyer from Iran. Anyways, I've decided come what may, silent is golden. And also come what may, I will not let anyone get me down. I will rise up like that bird, was it a vulture, that comes out of the ashes? Haan, bus I will be like that only from now on.

So, ever so silently and ever so determinedly, I put on The Old Bag's emeralds waala guluband, Janoo's grandmother's kimkhaab ki sari and my golden Jimmy Choo heels and went to the grand wedding in which they've replicated that famous French chatto, Where Sigh, right here in the middle of Lahore. But I took the precaution of taking a tiny corner of my sari ka pulloo and clenching it in my teeth like Zeenat Amman does in that olden times ki film, *Satnam Shivam Sundaram*, in which her face is burnt like a cinder all down one side but the hero (I think so it was Shashi Kapoor) never finds out because she keeps that burnt side of her face covered with her sari ka pulloo.

January 2009

Acute shortage of CNG cripples Lahore
Butterfly takes a short rest from partying

Never thought I'd say this but thanks God Muharram is here and we have a ten day brake from shaadis, parties vaghera. Honestly, this time tau I thought that I'd die on my feet, so hectic, so hectic it was. Pehlay tau I went and got that stuppid sa cold store on my lip, then my stomach ran and ran as if it was some Olympick marathong runner from Kenya or Somalia or whatever other country these thin black runner types come from. And oopar say I also got the flue. I swear my scenes take kar kar keh my insides have all rotted away. Despite of that I attended every shaadi, every party that I was invited to because being the selfless, thoughtful, considerable person that I am, I didn't want anyone to feel let down and disappointed because of a no-show from me. Itna mein, honestly, karti hoon na logon kay liye keh poocho hi na.

Before Muharram started, 12th December was the last day I had a meal at home. Lunch it was, I remember as clearly as if it was yesterday, and Flopsy, Mulloo, Jeeno and all had come. We sat in the patio and had shawarmas from Cock and Cow, na. So delish they are but unfortunately full of cholesteroils which go and clock up all your arteries and give you heart attack. Par chalo, once in while it's okay.

So nowdays I'm taking it easy and de-stressing. Or so I tell myself but not a moment of de-stress I get. Yesterday I went with Miskeen the driver to Mummy's and he asked me when he was dropping me if he could go and get CNG for the car while I sat with her. I said okay. But I sat and sat and sat and he didn't come. We bitched about the whole world and still he didn't come. I called his mobile three, four times but it was off.

'Ho na ho, he's run off with your car,' Mummy said. Aik tau she's also such a bloom and doom type person, na. The internal pessimist. 'You mark my words. He's gone. I told you before also not to get naukars from your husband's village. But did you listen? Never in a thousand years. By this time he's probably crossing the boarder into Afghanistan where your car will be sold twenty times over before you've even managed to inform the police. What's the point of calling his mobile? Might as be well calling Osama bin Laden for all the respond you are going to get.'

'Oho Mummy,' I said, 'aik minute tau please chup bhi karien. I'll call Janoo and find out if he knows anything.'

'As if that husband of yours ever knows anything! Might as well call Obama for all the respond you are going to get!'

Just then there was a knock on the door and Mummy's bearer came in and said that my car had arrived. When I asked Miskeen why it had taken him so long to come back he said that because guvmunt are rationing CNG for cars because they have to save it for factories, also he'd had to go to five petrol stations before he got some CNG and then also he'd had to cue for forty minutes before they filled him up. And because of electricity load shedding at home he hadn't been able to sir charge his phone properly and so it had run out of battery, which was why he couldn't take my call.

Dekho zara! No bijli, no gas, no petrol and now no CNG also. On top Hyper Star has also run out of avocadoes! Yeh koi mulk hai?

February 2009

Civilian peace mission returns from India
Butterfly appears in society magazine

Again peace mission has gone and come back from India. Again they didn't take me. Dekho zara! All these bore, bore types went instead. NGO wallahs and human writes wallahs and journalists and politicos aur pata nahin kaun kaun. No wonder they have come back with their own faces. No wonder Indians are still not talking to us. I wouldn't do sullah with such bore types either, baba. That'll teach them to take more interesting people next time.

Honestly, mein hoti tau I would have had all the Indians eating out of my hand in two sticks. I would have talked about how even our farishtas don't know who Ajmal Kasab is and how I am so much believer of Pak–Hind dosti, and how we should all follow example of Dawood Ibrahim and Javed Miandad who've got their bacchas married despite of being from opposite sides of the boarder. Then I would have makkhan lagaoed them by telling them how my favourite book is *The Wide Tiger* (which I haven't read but hear has won the Noble Prize) and how my favourite film is *Slump Dog*

Millionaire (which I didn't like but hear is going to win the Oscar) and I would have said how true their depictation of India is and how world is saying hai, what a lovely, neat and clean place India is and how much of human they have and how much I admire them. Then I would have gone shopping to Khan Market and I would have won over each and every shopkeeper by giving him best custom he's ever had. Bus. Peace achieved.

And all this time while I've been making my Pak–Hind dosti plans, Janoo has been blubbing in front of TV watching Barrack and Mitchell Obama's inoculation.

'This is historic!' he said again and again like a struck record to poor Kulchoo whom he forced to watch the whole thing on CNN.

'This is bore,' I whispered from behind my latest copy of *Good Times* which has a picture of me on page four, top right hand corner, third from left. I'm the dazzling one in blue. Royal blue, not light blue. In light blue is my best friend Mulloo, who's looking in that picture like a blue whale—the largest animal that's ever inhabited earth, as Kulchoo was reading to me from his homework yesterday. Bigger even than the tyrannosaurus sex.

Haan, so Mitchell Obama in yellow frock and green shoes. Okay, I suppose. Vaisay mein hoti tau I would have added some more blings. You know jhoomar ya solitaires ki bangles ya guluband ya rani haar or something.

'Maybe Mitchell Obama should appoint me as her fashion adviser,' I said aloud, lowering the corner of my *Good Times*.

Both father and son ignored me. Luckily I am immunized against them. And aur bhi luckily, tension tau mein leti hi nahin. So I went back happily to my *Good Times*, to page four, top right hand corner, third from left . . .

March 2009

Three family members killed in botched burglary
Aunty Pussy loses her gold buttons

Such a big phudda at Aunty Pussy's, na. Mummy called at crack of noon to tell me. Apparently some jewellery of Aunty Pussy's had gone missing. Since chors came to her house a few years ago and made Jonkers open the safe at gun point she'd stopped putting anything mehnga in it. Now she just keeps about ten thou there in case chors come again and do her insults and give her two tight slaps for not having enough inside her safe. Instead she keeps her pearls inside her court shoes or her diamond studs in her medicines ka drawer or her rings with the common pins inside her desk. Janoo's sister, Psycho, keeps her jewellery in the freezer and the other day she nearly threw an emeralds ki string into the pulao thinking it was frozen peas. Unfortunately she realized in time and fished them out.

Haan, so Aunty Pussy was going to a lunch and she opened her underwears ka drawer for her gold buttons and guess what? They'd gone. She said she looked inside bras, underwears, wests, socks–shocks, everything, but found nothing. She called

Mummy and shrieked down the phone that someone had taken her teen tolay kay gold buttons and that she was sure it was the sweepress who'd started dressing much too fashiony recently and that she was going to give her straight away to police. Mummy asked her if she was sure that she'd put her buttons there only. And Aunty Pussy said that she'd tucked them with her own hands into the left cup of her Marks and Spencer ki cross your heart firm control skin coloured bra. So Mummy told her in any case to have a look at her other favourite hiding places 'because you know, na, Pussy, that you have many more hiding places than your average Begum' but Aunty Pussy shouted at Mummy that what did she think she was? Demented? And she said that Mummy might have a hundred hiding places but that she, Pussy, only had two. And Mummy said that if you are going to be like that, Pussy, then I'm not talking to you and shut up the phone. And then she called me and I advised to Mummy that zamana was very kharaab and unless Aunty Pussy wanted to be murdered in her own bed at night she shouldn't give the servants to the police. And Mummy said I should tell her myself and I told her ji I'm not her servant ji and Mummy said that if I was going to talk like that then she wasn't going to speak to me and shut up her phone.

Anyways, because Aunty Pussy would never pass up on a free lunch, despite of the loss of her gold buttons, she got ready and as she was putting on her shoes, she felt some things inside her right shoe and turned it upside down and out fell her buttons. Or at least that's what she said when she called me to tell Mummy but I told her to tell her yourself only and she said I'm not your servant ji and shut up her phone.

April 2009

Food inflation at 12 per cent
Kulchoo goes vegetarian

Aik tau I'm surrounded by cracks. First I had to cope up with Janoo, crack number one, and oopar say now I have Kulchoo, crack number two.

One day while we were sitting having lunch—mutter keema, fish kebabs and daal gosht—Kulchoo suddenly pushed his plate away and announced that from today only he was going to become a vegetable, sorry, I mean vegetarian.

'I can't continue eating my fellow beings,' he said. 'My conscience won't allow it.'

First tau I thought he meant that he'd become, Allah na karay, a cannibal. You know, two years ago there was this long story in the papers about a family of poors who lived near a graveyard and because they couldn't afford meat, they would dig up freshly buried people and eat them only. Imagine! How greedy, no?

But mashallah say Kulchoo tau comes from affording family. He's a khaata peeta. So immediately I thought to myself keh he can't be like those graveyard kay poors. But still he'd said his 'fellow beings' and when someone says fellow beings you don't imagine kutta billas, do you?

But Janoo understood immediately—I told you na, he's an Oxen which is what BA wallahs from Oxford are called—and so while I was quietly eating my khaana, Janoo and Kulchoo started this long bore conversation about whether it was morally right to eat animals and whether it was okay to breed cattles on land that could be used for growing crops and other stuppid, stuppid things like that.

'Acchha bhai, phir tum nay khana kya hai?' I asked Kulchoo.

'Vegetables, daal, rice, roti,' he said.

So being a loving mother, that night I had a proper vegetarian meal cooked for my baby: saag gosht, aloo gosht, bhindi gosht and chicken ka pulao. But when Kulchoo came to the table, instead of being happy and saying thank you Mummy, he tau sighed and said he couldn't eat any of it.

'Why, baba?' I asked. 'There's bhindi, there's aloo, there's saag.'

'Yes, with gosht, gosht, gosht.'

'Chalo, eat pulao then.'

'But that's got chicken.'

'Hai, but chicken is so light, it's almost a vegetable.'

So then traitor Kulchoo turned to Janoo and said, 'She doesn't get it, does she?'

'Just cook him some vegetables—plain bhindi, daal, aloo, gobi. Shouldn't be so hard,' Janoo said to me.

So that evening I had aloo gobi and mutter gajjar made for him. But instead of daal, I told the cook to make mullah gutawny soup. Acchha change ho jaye ga, I thought. But that night Kulchoo ate the veggies but majaal hai that he touched even a drop of soup. When I asked him why he said it had animal stock.

You know, I've heard of this religious group of ladies in India, for some reason they all have the same name. They are all called Jane. So these Janes, na sirraf they don't eat meat, chicken, fish vaghera but they also don't eat potatoes or garlics and onions and all because they think they are also alive. I wouldn't go so far as to say that a murghi is my cousin sister or even my fellow being, but chalo, itna mein agree karti hoon that chickens are living things because I have seen them run and sqwauk and eat with my own eyes. But I've yet to see a potato run or an onion sqwauk. But then a lot of people—like nearly all our Sharkpur kay servants—have seen ghosts also which, thanks God, I have never seen. So just because I haven't seen something doesn't mean it doesn't happen. Maybe in India, and khaas taur pey in the south which they say is almost another country, maybe over there, there really are talking potatoes and flying carrots. One has to keep an opened mind, no?

So for two minutes I thought maybe Kulchoo has also seen these things and become a Jane. But then I reminded myself that my Kulchoo, he's not a girl so he can't be a Jane. Hai, thanks God for small messies.

Anyways, for next four, five days we all had just bore vegetables, kabhi gajjar tau kabhi gobi, tau kabhi karela, tau kabhi teenda, until I felt I was becoming a vegetable myself. You see, problem was that Janoo declared that vegetarianism was so much more healthy for the health—less cholesteroils vaghera—and so he also did copying of Kulchoo and started eating veggies. Reh gayee mein, and I was too embarrassed to say keh bhai, mein gosht kay beghair zinda nahin reh sakti. But honestly, I was craving meat so much, so much keh every day, I used to sneak out just before dinner time and quietly have a chicken shawarma from Cock and Cow. And then I'd rush home, brush my teeth, eat a few mints and sit at the dining table and pick at the saag.

But, thanks God, after two weeks the cook came to see me and said keh he wanted to give his designation.

'Bhai, why?' I asked.

Because, he said, he was sick and tired of cooking food for poors.

'When I came to work for you I thought I was going to cook in a rich house and I could show you what, what I could do, biryanis and koftas and mutanjan and pasanday, instead of which din raat I am making daal and aloo. This is my insult. This much tau even an anari cook can cook.' So he said he was leaving for some asal rich home where they knew what nice food was.

So I rushed into Janoo's study and I said to Janoo that look what you and Kulchoo have deduced me to.

'Even the khansamah is calling me a hungry, naked, fake khandani.' And then I told him everything.

And Janoo said, 'There's no reason why he can't cook meat for you. I know how much you want to support Kulchoo and I know what a big sacrifice it will be for you to eat meat again, but I insist that for the sake of keeping on the cook, you do so.'

So while Kulchoo and Janoo chew on their carrots and munch on their moolis, I make the supreme sacrifice every day of eating korma and biryani and haleem and koftas. Honestly, nobody told me mother hood was going to be this hard.

May 2009

Massive army action against Taliban in Swat
Butterfly takes a stand

Janoo is alighting candles in Zahoori Bagh outside BM (oho, Badshahi Mosque nahin hai?). When he told me he was going there for alighting candles, I thought must be something to do with load shedding. But no. It was a do with civil society, against Talibans, na. Aajkal whenever the extremists burst a bomb and fifty people die, civil society wallahs, they at once fight back by alighting candles. The poors, I mean those who can't afford generators, they alight candles in their homes but we khaata peeta civil society types, we do it in public places only and also only when we want to went our rage. So I also went along, me and Mulloo and Tony and Mummy and Aunty Pussy and Jonkers and Fluffy and Nina and their husbands, Anwar and Pappu. We also alighted candles and did slogans against them, not against Anwar and Pappu, but against Talibans. Lots of people there were. And all jaana pehchaana, khaata peeta types, which makes it twice as important.

Next day I went to Mall Road also in my Channel ki dark glasses and Prada kay shoes and did jaloos which was a bit have hazard, I'm sorry to say. All here and there it was. So after we'd jaloosed and done our bit against the Talibans, Mulloo and me and Fluffy got into our cars and came straight home and switched on our TVs to see if we'd come in them. We had! The camera stayed on me for full five seconds. Obviously, Mulloo, jealous type that she is, tried to jostle me aside so she could also come on TV but I stood my ground. I mean why was I there after all? To take a stand of course. So I took my stand.

Vaisay honestly, aik tau these Talibans also! So much of panic they have spread, na. Every day, girls' schools getting dhumkees of bomb attack. And beardo weirdos stopping women and threating to slice their arms off if they wear sleeveless again and throwing acid in their faces if they wear jeans. Imagine! As if Pakistan belongs to them! And we are their slaves! Thanks God the army is finally beating them up. So over dew. I hope so now they'll finish them off once and for all and not do a little bit of maar kuttai and then go quietly from behind and do sullah with them again and as a make up present give them another chunk of the country.

'Here, take Swat. And here's Kohat. Want Mardan also? Chalo, koi baat nahin, take that also. Have all of the province. After all it's yours only.'

Vaisay about one thing I'm very depress and that's the poors who are caught in the across fire. Talibans are apparently not letting them leave. And I'm also very sad about all those who've had to leave their homes. After all if I had to leave my lovely Gulberg kothi with its lovely lawns and verandahs and servants' quarters vaghera, I would also be heart broken. So now we are raising funds for the refugees from the fighting like we did for the earthquake victims. Janoo was saying we'll have to make appeals to UN wallahs to help us.

'Kyoon ji?' I said. 'Hum sub kiss liye hain?'

And at once I called up Mulloo and Fluffy and all and we called around and made a big collection. So many people gave. And tomorrow we are sending it to Swat for them. And then the day after we are doing another big collection. Least we can do, nahin . . . ?

June 2009

Taliban flee Swat
Butterfly plans her summer vacation

It's that time of year. When we choose where to go for summers. When Janoo and I do tiffs and then stop talking altogether. First he says where he wants to go. I pretend to listen carefully, then I tell him it's all wrong and he is crack. Then I talk about where I want to go and Janoo says what rot. Then bus tiff ho jati hai.

So this year I told him I wanted to go to Harrods in July.

'England, you mean?' he said.

'Same difference,' I said.

'Not quite,' he said.

'Don't be bore,' I said. Aik tau he always has to take off baal ki khaal.

'Anywhere else? And don't say Dubai or Singapore.'

'Sacks Fifth Avenew?'

'You mean New York.'

'Aik tau you also take off a baal's khaal,' I said.

'We always go to New York and London. I want to go somewhere new,' he said.

I quickly did duas under my breaths in case he says Africa or some other jungly place like that.

'Thailand?'

'No. Baby went there last month and if we go now she'll think we're doing her cheating.'

'Okay, how does Italy grab you? Rome? Florence?'

'Uff Allah. All those bore, bore museums and those old, broken buildings. What's that really broken down place called right in the centre of Rome? Haan, the Foreign. But maybe we can stop there for two days and I can get some bags shags, shoes vooze.'

'No, let's go to Shanghai,' said Janoo quickly. 'I hear it pulsates with energy.'

'China waala Shanghai keh Mr Lee ka Shanghai?'

'China waala Shanghai,' said Janoo. 'Not Mr Lee's restaurant in Gulberg.'

'Just asking, baba. Anyways, answer is no.'

'Why, for God's sake?'

'Fluffy went last year and she said the food is inaddible. All pheeka, pheeka, slippery jaisa. She says they don't even know how to cook beef and chilli. Rather go to Mr Lee's Shanghai where at least you get proper Chinese chicken sweet and sour. And also their rice is all stuck together, not like ours, all nicely separate, separate.'

'Any other reason?' Janoo sighed.

'I've had a fight with Linda.'

'Who in God's name is Linda?'

See? Only this much interest he takes in my life.

'Linda Chong, baba. My Chinese hairdresser. If I go to

China she'll feel that I've forgiven and forgotten and that things are chunky dory between us. So to keep Linda in her place, no China.'

'Let's just stay at home then,' Janoo said wearily.

I swear I keep telling you, it's me only who's done guzara with him all these years. See what a buddi rooh stay-at-home he is?

July 2009

Twenty-three militants killed in Dir, Swat
Butterfly finds London full of desis

Aaj kal hum London aye huay hain, na. Who? Me, Janoo and Kulchoo. Who else? Vaisay there's lots of elses here also. Who, who? Well, for starters, Salman and Sara Shoaib, bhai, voh diamond waali Sara, you know who has her own jewellery ka business in Singapore. Janoo calls her the rock chick. And then Sana—uff baba, Hashwani—and Sadaf Munir and Hussain Haqqani and Farahnaz Ispahani—oho bhai, Hussain Haqqani who is Asif Zardari ka ambassador in Washington VC only—and Aban and Kairas Kabraji—un ke tau children live here, na—and my friends Naila and Sohail Malik and Snooky and Popity and their daughters and daughters-in-law and Mouse and Poppy also.

The hot hang out is a restaurant called Chipriyani. Last week there were five full tables of desis there. First tau I thought the restaurant was belonging to a Sindhi family. You know, their names also all end with 'ani', na. Shivdhisani, Mulchandani, Dadlani and Whateverani. But now I think so it is Italian. Janoo says their names also end with 'ani'. No wonders, I said, Armani is Armani. Yeh hotay hain advantages of being an Oxen. You know all these important, important things that nobody else knows. Anyways, this Chipriyani has all these nice, nice, rich, rich desis coming. And Janoo says at the other tables there are Russian Oily Garks with their six foot blonde bazooka girl friends in their nine inch sky scrapper heels and nine inch long nails. And the desis? They wear big, big designer ki sunglasses and big, big designer ke handbags and big, big blonde stripes in their hair and big, big lips full of cellulite.

I also went with Furry and Bobby Bhai and at the next table two couples were exchanging jokes, the men slapping their thighs and guffawing and the women giggling into their napkins. 'Javani aur burhapay mein kya farq hai? Javani mein mobile mein haseenon kay number hotay hain, burhapay mein hakeemon kay.' Then they all laughed loudly, loudly.

Sales are almost finished. Not that sales mein kabhi kuch milta hai vaisay. I think so they put all their do number ka maal in them. But yesterday I found this lovely black jumper with diamante ke sequences all over the neck like a big haar, na. From Gucci for three hundred pounds only. Reduced from four fifty. My bad kismet that the label inside the neck was torn. But I'll get my Filipina to stitch it back when we get home and I'll wear it to Sunny's immediately. I know summers hain but she has three splits in her sitting and it's like a fridge inside.

Everyone was saying in Lahore keh west mein barha slum aya hua hai and things are so bad for the goras that they are going around with begging bowls. Zara bhi nahin. All restaurants are full. All shops are full. All streets are khacha khuch. Vaisay if you look closely half the customers are Arabs and the other half us desis, mostly Indians, to be honest, but they are also desis after all. Just shows that Allah loves us best. That's why slum never comes on us.

August 2009

Three sanitary men die of suffocation
Butterfly finds lizard in bedroom

I'm writing this in PIA flight from London to Lahore. Business class, obviously. And honestly, despite of smell of garlic and haldi that all PIA planes have, I tau say home sweet home, baba. Can't wait to get home, yaar. I've spent a hole month in London shopping and meeting sheeting all my nice, nice, rich, rich friends from home. (Who wants to meet bore goras with their long marsiyas about credit crunch except crack Janoo who hooks up with all his old Oxen friends?) Anyways, London shops, especially Harrods and Selfridges tau are zabardast and also after Lahore ki heat, London ka weather is so totally nice with its thin, thin rain and its cool, cool breeze and its over casted skies and also Royal China and Zoo Ma and Chipriyani are to dye for and Daniel Galving jaisa tau hairdresser, who does Madonna, Kylie and me, is just tabahi and Nell Gwin house in Chell Sea with its Filipina maid three times a week is my second home but only second, na. Why? Because underneath my sophisty appearance and my glam looks I'm just a seedhi saadhi patriotic homely type, na.

My real home tau is Lahore where I never have to make a bed or boil a cattle to make tea or pull my own curtains or top up my own phone or fetch a glass of water or put milk in Kulchoo's serial. Can't wait to get home and be greeted at the airport with the admi who comes to meet us at the airport (he stands just outside the plane only) and collect our luggage and do all the bore paper work while we just sail home in our own car and walk into our lovely shiny kothi with the ACs already humming and be met by my shweet shi maid who does all the unpacking and who I don't have to thank ten, ten times like all those sarrhial Filipinas in London who have so many hairs and braces keh taubah! And I get to eat ghar ka khaana—daal, chaaval and mutter keema, my absolute fave. Now I'm going to sleep under my pashmina so please excuse, na. See you in Lahore. Byeee!

Uff taubah, that stupid admi who's supposed to whisk us out of passport control and immigration vaghera isn't here and we're having to cue just like the cattle class types. So humiliating. I just told Janoo to fire him next time he sees him and Janoo said he's not our naukar. He works for guvmunt. Well, tomorrow I'm going to call guvnur himself and tell him to fire him and after that I'm going to fire Janoo. And now we're having to wait in the luggage hall with the porter to collect our luggage while all our friends from biz class sailed out ages ago leaving their admis to do all that. Honestly! Talk about bezti. And all these Pakis push and shove so much with their bloody trolleys unlike the goras who quietly get into cue and wait.

Got home two hours later and guess what? Maid is ill!

Sent message that she's got malaria. Jhooti jaisi! Wait till she comes back. I'll fire her on the spot. And generator is not working and phone is not working and our bathroom got flooded in the rains and it's still so bloody hot and damn fool cook thought we were coming tomorrow so he hasn't made lunch and to top it all there's a chip killi in my room. I hate my house. I hate my servants. I hate the guvmunt. I hate Lahore. Hai, London, I miss you . . .

September 2009

Country observes Ramadan al Mubarik
Butterfly converses in Arabic

'Mashallah. Ramadan al Kareem is here,' I said to Janoo.

There was no reply from behind the wall of newspaper on the sofa. Maybe he's died or something, I thought. After all, he's been behind that wall all morning, maybe even from night before, with no movement, no talk, nothing. But if he'd, God forbid, passed away then the newspaper would have fallen, no?

'I said, thanks be to Almighty Allah, the fasting month is here again. Remember, Ramadan al Kareem?' I said, raising my voice like I do for poor old Aunty Dodo, Mummy's great-aunty, who wears a hearing aid but never switches it on to save on the battery.

'Don't have to shout. I can hear you loud and clear,' came Janoo's voice from behind the newspaper.

'Then why don't you reply first time, haan? Making me repeat and repeat for nothing.'

'Because I don't understand Arabic, still less speak it.'

'So who's speaking Arabic, for God's sake?'

'You are.'

'Me?'

'Yes, you.'

'No.'

'Yes.'

'No.'

Silence.

'What do you mean Arabic?' I asked.

'In Urdu we call it Ramzan. Just Ramzan.'

'Ramadan al Kareem sounds more holy, more respectful.'

'No, it just sounds more Arabic, ya wife.'

'Don't call me ya wife.'

'But surely it sounds more respectful?'

I trounced out of the room. No point khappaowing your head with a crack. Anyways, my patients tau totally goes when I am fasting.

At iftaar time we were sitting down at the table. Me and Kulchoo and Janoo. Honestly, vaisay sometimes I don't recognize Janoo without a newspaper on his face. He looks so naked without it. Like Mulloo without her foundation or Sunny without her false lashes or Aunty Pussy without her penciled eyebrows. Anyways, to get back to the iftaari, Kulchoo and Janoo had been exchanging looks through out while I loudly, loudly told the servants that because it was the holy month of Ramadan al Kareem and because ours was a respectful Muslim household, and because I knew that they were also fasting I wouldn't make them serve us first. Because I am like that only. Kind. Considerable. Selfless. They could go and open their fasts with their samosas and chaat in the kitchen while we did the same (but with more goodies) in the dining room and then they could have some tea, relax a bit and then come and give us khaana. Okay?

So when the servants left, I asked Kulchoo if he'd like some tea.

'Shaay? La, shukran, ya umme,' he said.

'Chai?' I repeated.

'La, ya umme,' said Kulchoo, helping himself to pakoras while Janoo covered his twitching mouth with a napkin.

And then, 'The lahm's a bit pongy al-yom, ya umme? Still, mustn't complain during Ramadan al Kareem. Ya Allah wouldn't approve.'

'Don't think I don't know what you two are up to, ji,' I hissed at Janoo.

'Me? What have I done now?' asked Janoo, acting all innocent jaisa.

'This Arabic sharabic. It's all your doing.'

'My doing?'

'La, ya umme,' cut in Kulchoo. 'Min fadlak, don't blame ya abu.'

'I'm not going to sit here and allow you two to lagao my record,' I said, getting up and flinging my napkin on the table.

'Raheem!' I shouted to the bearer. 'Bring my dinner to my room. At once.'

'But what about Ramadan al Kareem, ya umme?' called Kulchoo after me. 'What about our observant Muslim household? Our selflessness, our virtue, ya umme? Ya umme?'

October 2009

Turkish PM, Erdogan, visits Islamabad
Butterfly blames Taliban for melted chocolates

Hai, bechari Furry. Itna phudda hua hai na uss keh saath in Isloo, keh bus. Bhai, you know, na, that her daughter-in-law had a baby boy last week, and that also after three girls one after another. Furry tau I think so had quietly, quietly even started shopping for daughter-in-law number two, because as she says, 'I tau have only one child and he can't remain childless.' She has two daughters also but them she doesn't count, although she's fond of them and everything. And also she has two granddaughters but they also don't count, na. Anyways, the long awaited baby boy has finally come— they've named him Sikander and because his father is called Aazam, baby's full name is Sikander-e-Aazam. So naturally, they wanted to celebrate. But because this is the mother's fourth Sea Section and because she nearly died this time from complications and is still in hospital, they thought we'll do a tabahi function later when she comes out but in mean time, milnay vaalon ko mithai tau send karein, na.

So they got chocolate flown in from Dubai because no

affording, sophisty type would be seen dead distributing luddoos anymore. Sooo last millennium. The chocolate was all hand made but obviously they couldn't send it in its own car board boxes, because that looks dull, so they had these cute say blue silk pouch type things made with golden tassels and put five, five chocs in each with a card saying 'In honour of Sikander-e-Aazam, world conqueror'.

But worst luck. Turkish Prime Minister, what's his name, Astrakhan or Ardogan or something, he arrived in Isloo just then. Now the guvmunt as you know is scared skiff keh about where Talibans will strike next and fearing keh Sri Lankan cricket team waala haal Turks ka na ho jaye, they closed down hole of Isloo to protect Turks ka PM, Mr Astrakhan. I swear you couldn't take three steps without getting stopped by police at a check post and being searched in places you didn't even know you had.

Khair, Furry sent out three hundred blue silk pouches in her silver Merc with her driver to deliver round Isloo and because of fear of zamana he kept his windows up (if your window is down, they put a gun to your head and straight away take your phone, na) and because of fear of Furry who is a little bit kanjoos, he didn't dare switch on the car AC and because of all the road blocks he left the house at 9 a.m. and didn't get back till 9 p.m. and all that time the chocs quietly melted onto the cards and got stuck up to the blue silk and when people opened their pouches they found a small sa brown puddle and a card that they could only read this much 'am world conqueror' and everyone thought, 'Haw, who is this cheapster?'

Next day poor Furry sat by her phone all day waiting for thank you and mubarik ki calls which didn't come. Finally, her bestie, Twinkle, called her and told her and that also only because Twinkle had gone shopping with Furry and chosen the exact right shade of blue for the silk pouches, na, and so when hers was delivered to her she knew keh yeh kiss kay ghar say aya hai. So poor Furry became victim of her own kanjoosi and haalaats. Honestly, how many more ways are Talibans going to make us suffer . . .

November 2009

India arrests thirty Pakistani fishermen
Butterfly dabbles in housework

What I want to know is this. Why shareef, khandani, sophisty, parha likha, well knowned, khaata peeta types like us, who've been there hundred, hundred times, and lived there in our own big, central London kay flats, are not getting UK ka visa and every Sri Lankan or chalta purza Filipina maid, who hasn't even gone beyond Faislabad, is? What it is that they have that we don't? Haan? It's not money, it's not bagground, it's not English (speaking waali, I mean), it's not getup, it's not looks. Then what it is? When I asked Janoo, he said a good employer.

'What do you mean, "a good employer"?'

'Correction,' he said. 'I should have said a well-connected employer.'

'You mean if I was a maid in the house of say Asif Zardari or Shaukat Aziz I could get a London ka visa just like that?'

'Just like that.'

Haw, I thought to myself. How unfair. Just for sitting around on your bottoms all day in the house of Asif Zardari

71

or Shaukat Aziz you get a UK ka visa just like that. And here's poor Jonkers having to do bio matric tests and being interrorated and being made to wait for thousands of years just for one month ka sarrha hua visiting visa. So I said to Janoo keh banda phir maid hi bun jaye, nahin?

'Why don't you try?' he said.

'Are you challenging me? You think so, I can't do it? Haan?'

'Why don't you just try it for a day and then tell me whether you think they have a better deal?' he said.

So today I'm dabbling myself in housework. First I opened the curtains. Then I opened the windows. Then I gave myself a bath and even took my clean clothes out of the cupboard and put my dirty clothes in the dirty clothes ki basket. Honestly, work is so good for you. Then I made my own hair. Then I seedha karoed the sofa cushions. Then I pulled the bed cover straight. I hate it when Basheeran doesn't get the stripes straight. Phir phone came. I picked it up with my own hands, without even knowing if it was going to be for me or for someone else. It was for Kulchoo. So I shouted up the stairs, 'Phone has come for you, Kay darling. Pick up.'

After that I went into lounge where Janoo had left his newspaper on an armchair. I picked it up and put it neatly on the table. One photograph in its frame was a bit lock sided so I seedha karoed that also. Then I stood back to survey my handy work. Then I sat down and made a few phone calls. Then I saw that one flower in the vase was drooping. Honestly, servants don't even see this much. So I took it out and threw it in the waste paper basket. Then I went into sitting room. There was a fly buzzing around. When it sat down on the sofa, I rolled up a magazine and squatted it. Then I disposed off it myself only with the magazine. Then I washed my hands. Then I dried them with the towel. Then, baba, I got very tired so I lay down on my bed and I thought that this maid vaid business is very bore. I swear, to hell with UK ka visa. And anyways, everything you get in Harrods you get in Mall of the Emirates also. So who cares? I'd much rather be a khandani type who goes to Dubai rather than a fly squatter in Musharraf's London ka flat.

December 2009

Load shedding of up to four hours a day from December
Butterfly winters in Dubai

Uff, such fun I'm having in Dubai. Ji haan. I'm here for Christmas only. And I've also got Janoo and Kulchoo with me. Actually, it is because of Kulchoo that we came. You know, na, that he's paagal about architecture, particularly sky scrappers, and his most best sky scrapper is Burj ul Arab in Dubai, which he tells me is made by British architect called Sir Normal Foster. So anyways, Kulchoo had been doing so much of work for his end of year exams (he came first, natch!) and after that he got really bad flue and Janoo said he was runned down and needed a holiday and so he asked Kulchoo where he would like to go and Kulch, shweetoo jaisa, itna sensitive hai, he didn't say bore Sharkpur, and he didn't say more bore Salt Range, he said, 'Dubai to see Burj ul Arab.' And so Janoo immediately booked tickets (if I'd said Dubai for Mall of Emirates, you think so he'd have gone? Never!) and so here we are in a fab hotel on Jumeirah Beach.

I tau love our hotel, baba. It's right on the beach and I

think so it has a thousand rooms (we've got a sweet, natch) and everywhere in the lobby there are cute say plastic kay Santa Claws and rain deers and elves vaghera. And jhooti snow. And every morning when I go down for my bouquet breakfast (muffins aur bagels aur halal sausages and smoked salmon and eggs aur kya kya) they are playing 'Jingles Bells'. Every morning without fail. I think so it's a recording. So cute.

And it's so trendy and cool, na, with all these tall busty blondes in short skirts and high heels with their short dark Arab husbands lurking around in dark corners, being all lovey dovey. And I said to Janoo, 'Dekho, you're constantly saying Gulf Arabs are so backwards and yet they have all these Swedish mems as wives. I think so they're all here for their honeymoons.' And he said, 'They're neither wives nor Swedish. They're Russian.' And then I noticed that so many signs in the hotel, they were all in Russian. I think so they must be liking Russians here.

I think so we must be the only desis staying in our hotel. Baaki sub, they are goras. All day they lie flat on their backs in their swimming costumes, gleaming with oil, by the pool. Like crocodiles in Kulchoo's nature books who lie all day on river banks in Africa. You know me, I never make personal comments but some of the men, particularly the fat bald ones, they wear such small chaddis that they might as well not bother and some of them are the colour of carrot halwa. And also, if I was as old and wrinkly as some of the goris, I really wouldn't wear swim suit in public and voh bhi two pieces. Nothing personal vaisay.

Vaisay life here, na, it's just tabahi. Na koi dust and na koi fakirs and na koi poors and na koi smells and na koi flies and na koi in-laws and na koi dakoos and na koi bombs and na koi gutters and na koi pot holes either. Everything is saaf suthra and chup chaap and there are no trees so there are no leaves to sweep and no birds to sit in them and do potty on your car. There are no parks but who needs parks when you have nice cemented compounds and the servants, they are all smiley and polite and English speaking with no families and no bother. All my friends live in big, big houses with Filipinas and swimming pools and twenty-four hour bijli, and petrol is so cheap that they all leave their car engines running even when they hop out to do some quick shopping, like picking up a *Vogue* or a cartoon of milk. And the malls! And the restaurants! And the clubs! Uff, bilkull jannat, I tell you.

Janoo says they have no freedom and that I should try doing a protest jaloos here and see what happens to me. And I said, 'Bhai, what is there to protest about, haan? Am I crack that I would want to do a jaloos in jannat?' And then he said, 'You know also that they don't have elections?' And I said, 'Tau hum ko itni elections kar kay kya mil gya hai, haan?' Honestly, some time I think so Janoo's Oxen educations is totally wasted on him. Mujhay jana chahye tha to Brazen Nose college . . .

January 2010

Lahore welcomes the New Year with subdued festivities
Butterfly makes some New Year resolutions

I'm telling you from now only, so don't say afterwards that I keep secrets, but I'm turning over a new leave. So I've made a list of New Year revolutions:

1. Fight less with Janoo. Khair, that should be easy because up until last year we would fight and then two minutes later Janoo would say sorry and we'd make up and then three days later we'd fight again. So basically in one month I think so, we were fighting at least ten, twelve times. Now I've noticed Janoo doesn't do sullah so quickly, and why should I say sorry when I'm always right, so one fight is lasting four, five days. So already we're fighting only five, six times a month . . .

2. Loose twenty pounds. I know, I know keh it doesn't show but really I'm becoming a bit too hippy. Even my darzi's noticed. So I'm turning vegetarian because they say you loose lots of weight that way. So no more aloo gosht and nihari and mutton tikka for me. Instead only chicken and fish and prawns and lobster vaghera.

3. Give no safe heaven in my home to Janoo's family. No more Eid ka khaanas for his sisters, The Gruesome Twosome, no more iftaris for The Old Bag, no more annual dinners for his other paindu pastry distant type rellies who finger my silk curtains with their greasy paindu hands and ask, 'Hai, Baji, how much you paid for these, haan?' Bus, my patients has run out.

4. Take no tensions. See above.

5. Find new facial waali. Old one has bad breaths.

6. Wear only pinks and purples. My new smooth sayer, Mussarat Apa of D Block Model Town, has told me that I mustn't wear greys and browns. They bring me bad luck, na. And green tau is totally out because it's Mulloo's and the Taliban's favourite colour.

7. Buy some nice new rubies to go with my new pinks.

8. Visit places I've never seen before. Like Burj Khalifa in Dubai (it wasn't finished when I was there, na) and new Channel ki boutique in Singapore.

9. Take regular exercise. Like walking to dressing room myself to fetch a tissue instead of yelling to maid.

10. Doing Hajj. All the girls—Bobo, Baby, Fluffy, Flopsy— have been and have done some umras also for extra points from Allah Mian and now I feel so out of it when we meet at coffee parties because they show off so much about their special relationship with Allah. Like Pakistan does with China.

11. Start attending more darses. See above.

12. Give no chhuttis to servants. All last year itna mera advantage take kiya hai na in sub ne, keh bus don't even

ask. One month one's mother would pass away, next month the other's father. Bus, now I think so all my servants are, thanks God, orphans so all chhuttis khatam.

13. Persuade Mummy to give up on cheetah prints. So last decade.

14. Wake up early. At 11.30 instead of 12.

So bus, just leading simple saaf suthri life. Aur kya?

February 2010

Measles epidemic in Lahore
Butterfly prepares for the end of the world

I tell you qiamat is coming. How do I know? Because signs and systems are all there, baba. Strange, strange things are happening. First, big floods have come. Oho baba, not just to us—we tau are used to, Bangladesh, India, Philippines, us, China—but in God's favourite countries also, like France, England and Germany vaghera, who God never ever gets angry with. So you see it's not like before. And then, uss say bhi worst, Mulloo told me that the cat in her servants' quarters, it had two kittens and guess what? The billa who I think so was their daddy, it came along and ate them both. Zara imagine karo. Eating your own children. Now if this is not a sign of doom day then tell me what is?

And oopar say, my friend Maha, she told me that her sister-in-law's niece, Ayesha, she's mashallah say very khaata peeta because her husband owns three textile mills and they live in a huge marble mention in Faisalabad, guess what happened to her? She got attacked by her driver. Ji haan. With a car ka jack.

Suna hai, he got upset because he asked her for a lone of five thou because he had to pay rishwat to a head master to get his son into a free guvmunt school but Ayesha refused because she said she didn't believe in rishwat and second, because she said she had no money. And then she made the driver take her to the jeweller where she bought twelve fat gold bangles and bus, the driver suddenly lost it and lunged at her with a car ka jack when she came out with the bangles jangling on her bare arm. Socho zara.

Luckily he came to his senses and he didn't hit her and he dropped the jack himself only before other people came and grabbed him and now he's being tortured in the local jail by the police but what if he had harmed her? Makes your blood freeze, no?

Floods tau I can cope up with, because like I said just now only, we have become used to and in any case when floods come here they come only in far, far places like Sindh and poorish villages of Punjab vaghera and cats tau I've never kept but between you, me and the four walls, this servants thing has really frightened me. What if they all do an up rise against us, haan? I tau have returned all my jewellery to the bank, baba, even though it's party season and I've raised all their pays by a thou each and I've taken to locking my door from the inside when I go to sleep and also put a chair in front of it like they do in movies and I've also begged Kulchoo to do same to same but you know what aaj kal kay bacchay are like, na. So ziddi, so ziddi that don't even ask.

Our bearer's brother came to visit him yesterday. I refused to let him enter the house. Why? Because he had a beard and walked with a limp. Now what more proof do you need that he's a fundo and he's fought in Afghanistan where he's chopped off hundred, hundred heads, haan? Janoo shouted at me and said I'd gone insane. Better insane than beheaded, I said. But I haven't gone mad. I told you before also that strange things are happening.

March 2010

**Twelve killed and twenty-nine injured in bomb attack on
police intelligence centre, Lahore
Butterfly works on a CV for Kulchoo**

You know, na, that Kulchoo is only fourteen? And you also
know that his GCSEs are standing on top of his head. But
instead of studying he has to make up something called a See
Wee. Apparently a See Wee is a letter that says what, what
you have done and how zabardast you are. This is a part from
all your studies and tuitions of course. Suna hai foreign ki
universities are all very crazy about See Wees and American
universities tau won't even look at you if you don't have a See
Wee as long as Osama's beard.

Vaisay tau most students start making their See Wees
when they're doing their A levels only but some parents, you
know the chalaak cheater types like Maha and Jeeno, while
their kids are doing parhai, they are chori chori making their
kids' See Wees themselves only by pulling stings and doing
cheating. So the second I found out what those two were up
to, I immediately thought keh bhai, why Kulchoo should
be left behind, haan? Naturally Maha and Jeeno didn't say a

single word about how it is they who are doing their kids' See Wees—it's a bit like taking Botox kay injections, na, everyone does but no one admits.

Obviously I couldn't tell Janoo because he tau would have gone up in smokes that why must I be so competitive and why did I have to put pressure on Kulchoo and God knows what, what else, so instead I quietly went behind Janoo's backside and asked Jonkers all about See Wees because you know, na, that he also went to a foreign ki university called Hull or Dull or something.

Jonkers told me universities like kids who play music— God knows why but they do. For instant, if your child plays violin in an orchestra it gives him lots of marks. But we don't want mirasis in our family, na, thank you very much. And anyways, if I'd wanted Kulchoo to be a band master doing the gaana bajaana at weddings and restaurants I wouldn't have put him in a school like Aitchison which is just for khandanis and parha likhas.

Then he said keh sport wallahs are also welcomed with open arms and if I'm honest then I have to admit that Janoo was also very keen on Kulch becoming a swimmer or hockey player but, baba, I tau put my feet down when he was small only. Swimming makes you so black. Everyone would think he was a negro. And also hockey gives you heat stroke, bhai, playing in the sun like that in the afternoon. And also most of the hockey players in Pakistan's national team, I'm sorry to say, but they're not from our bagground, na. And really, I'm not a snob or anything, okay? When I say Kulch shouldn't play with them, I'm thinking of their own good, really. I mean, I wouldn't want them to mix up with Kulchoo and get inferiority complexion, na.

So I think so for sport I'll put Kulchoo into carom only. You can play araam say in your own air-conditioned lounge and also it's so civilized and khandani because you don't have to sweat or get out of breaths or be pushed and shoved or, God forbid, jump into dirty water with dirty bodies from the wrong baggrounds. I sent Miskeen the driver to Gander Sports on Mall Road to buy a nice big board and I've already had it set up in the lounge. Kulch can play with Miskeen only when he gets home from school. I've already told Miskeen to let Kulch win four games out of five. Five out of five would look greedy, na.

Then Jonkers said that social work carried lots of weights with college admission wallahs. So I sent my friend Paro of Paro's Perfect Parties (she's an event manager, na) a huge buffet of orchids and two jars of cream de la merde and she agreed to give Kulch a job for two weeks. But I had to tell her keh bhai, don't give my baby too much of tension, okay? After all he's not a naukar, you know? So she said she'd either get him laying out napkins at a khaana or alighting cake candles for a baccha log ki birthday party or maybe even helping choose the music. Nothing too tiring because after all, shweetoo jaan, he also has to go to school, na. But if you ask me, this will be the icing on his See Wee ka cake because, what work can be more social than event managing?

And lastly, Jonkers kehta tha keh if you have one, two articles published in newspapers or magazines vaghera then that makes very good expression on universities. So what I've done, I've asked a poorish unmarried cousin of mine from Daddy's side—poor thing, she's missed the ship because she's thirty-three already and dark also—but she's nice, quiet, bore type who's always keeping herself busy by sending articles to magazines. After doing hello hi on the phone for two seconds I asked her if she had any unpublished articles lying around just like that and she said keh haan, she finished one yesterday only. So I told her that I'm sending the driver round just now only with five thousand rupees for her and to please rub out her own name from top and put Kulchoo's in its place and hand the article over.

'But are you sure, Apa? I mean the article is about . . .'

'I don't care what the article's about. I want it fata futt. Okay?'

Uff, aik tau people do so much of faaltu chit chat. They just don't know what it is to be professional.

Then I called my friend Saniya who runs *Femina* magazine. (I know the name sounds like a sanitary towel but ub what to do?) She owes me a mota sa favour because I gave her my maid for two weeks when I was in Dubai and her maid had run away. So I told her that I'm sending this really nice piece that Kulchoo has done and please to print it in this week's issue only. Centre spread. So then I called Miskeen on his cell and told him keh bhai, don't come home, go straight forward to *Femina* office on backside of Dr Shamshad and give this brown lifafa into Saniya Bibi's hands only. Honestly, aulaad key liye what, what one has to do. Two hours later I got a call from Saniya.

'This article that Kulchoo has done, you know, na, that it's about his personal experience as a lifelong sufferer of acute PMT?'

April 2010

Shoaib and Sania wed in India
Butterfly outraged at missing wedding

Lo, itna mein look forward kar rahi thi, na, to Shoaib and Sania's wedding and they've gone and done it chup chup kar ke in some hotel in Hyderabad and that also India waala Hyderabad and not ours which belongs to MQM and is near Sucker in Sind. Spoil spots jaisay. For the last five days I've been following all their tamasha with Ayesha Siddiqui who says he dumped her because of her weight issues and the snatching of his passport and Sania's pictures in those little, little skirts (littler even than Jemima's) on the inner net.

One thing I discovered about Shoaib which I think so no one else knows is that he is not really a cricketer. It's true. Promise by God. I read it with my own eyes. You know in cricket there are only two types of players, even a child knows that. There are ballers and there are batters. And some times they all become catchers and fielders but vaisay tau they are just ballers and batters. Well, Shoaib is neither. Instead he is skipper. Ji haan, instead of doing balling and batting he skips. With rope. I told Janoo and Kulchoo over dinner and they both looked at each other and then covered their mouths with napkins. I must tell to this new cook not to put so much of spices in food. Unlike me, poor things they can't take, na.

Kulchoo says I've become a cyber stalker and Janoo asks why I am invested so heavily in this wedding business.

'Haw,' I said, 'mein ne kya investment kee hai, bhai? Not one anna even I've given. I'm not the one who is going to give them golden crowns when they reach Sialkot. I'm not the one who is paying for their wedding ki feast.'

Apparently they are going to have thousand guests and twenty-three main kay courses, including something called pathar kay kebab (I knew Indians were veggies but honestly, even committed vegetarians like cows and sheeps draw a line at stones and gravel vaghera). And also there are going to be seventeen deserts.

But I think so despite of making all that much prize money in Wimbledong Sania is a bit of a kanjoos makhi choos. Why? Haw, don't you know she wore her mother's twenty-five years old sari to the nikah? And he tau is even bigger kanjoos makhi choos because he is going to give Ayesha Rs 15,000 a month for chutkara money. Lo, 15,000 tau doesn't even cover for monthly kharcha on shampoo, soap vaghera. But maybe Indians use stones for that also . . .

May 2010

Wheat price up
Kulchoo's dog passes away

Today we had a funeral in our house. Before you ask, no such luck. The Old Bag is still alive and licking. No, it was Kaaloo, Kulchoo's black labradog who's gone and died. Dekho zara. What an ungrateful dog vaisay. I spent so much money on his injections and on his food (milk two, two times a day and meat one time, and that also small meat, mutton you know, not beef) that the servants would say that Kaaloo eats like a foreigner, meat and milk, and we eat like poor desis, roti and water. Vaisay servants you know, they are so ungrateful. After everything you do for them, they still grumble.

But foreigner tau Kaaloo was. A pure bread labradog from UK, from Kent which is some county over there. (I thought counties were wives of counts but Janoo says their counties are like our provinces, only smaller.) Anyways, his name not withoutstanding, Kaaloo was from Kent, UK. And as I told you before also, he was thorough bread gora with a shajra as long as Bahadur Shah Zafar's.

And Kulchoo also treated him like a proper gora saab. Not

once did he ever sleep outside. Taubah karo! Kaaloo slept in Kulchoo's air-conditioned room and if ever Kulchoo went to spend a few nights here or there, tau the servants were four bidden to switch off the AC in case Kaaloo Saab got hot flashes. I told to Kulchoo, I said he's not about to get hot flashes, darling, just because his father was from Kent. But Kulchoo wouldn't budge.

As usual Janoo also took his side. 'I'm glad Kulchoo takes his responsibilities seriously,' he said.

So many nakhras that dog had. Couldn't stand makhees, couldn't stand other dogs, couldn't stand banging doors. But in one thing he and I were one. He couldn't stand The Old Bag. Every time he heard her voice even he'd start growling. As our gardener from Sharkpur used to say, he was a 'siyana' dog.

In his last few days I spent so much money on the wet (oho baba, wetnery doctor) keh poocho hi na. Could have bought four, four joras from Body Focus for that much. But the wet was useless. In the end the fever took him. Kaaloo, not the wet. Kulchoo cried like a baby. Janoo rushed back from Sharkpur to comfort him and attend Kaaloo's funeral. He's buried on our backside in the garden. Our bedroom ki windows look out on his grave. Hai, vaisay can dogs haunt you?

June 2010

Zardari expresses concern over target killings
Butterfly bumps into Musharraf

Thanks God, we're in London. This time we've rented a flat
in Anusmore Gardens on the backside of Knightsbridge.
A grenade's throw from Harrods. Two bed, two bath.
Unfortunately sitting dining are one. But chalo, never mind.
At least I'm in London. We're here because Janoo's old friend
from Oxford, John Porter or Potter or Porker, I don't know
what (these goras have such strange names vaisay) is getting
married. He's Janoo's age and he's getting married now only.
Imagine, so aged! Anyways, it's to be a big party in his country
state in Norfuck.

Apparently he has a big sa house over there with dears in
the garden and a lake also. It's called Home Park. (Or was
it Hyde Park?) Anyways, whatever it is, it must be funny
living in a park, no, with people jogging past your window
and couples doing chummi chaati in your front lawn. We
are supposed to go, in fact that's why we're here, but I think
so at the last minute I'll make excuse and say I have measles
or plague or meaningitis or something because who can be

91

bothered to spend whole day talking to foreigners? So bore, no? After all, it's a full year since I've come to London and then for Janoo to expect me to meet foreigners while I'm here, it's just not fair, is it?

Haan, so what I have been up to for the last week that I've been here? Aik tau I've had a few GTs with my friends from Lahore and Karachi. Sunny's here and also Baby and Maha. I swear it was so nice to do gup shup after three full days of no goss at all. I tau was getting withdrawal systems. So that was just like Lahore ka scene. I miss Lahore ka scene so much because I'm a patriot, na.

Talking of patriots, Janoo's friend, an Indian called Ajit who was also from Brazen Nose College and now lives near Yoo Hoo beach in Bombay, took us to this place called Mark's Club which I think so used to belong to Mark Bully who was married to Jemima's mother, Anna Bell, before she married Jimmy Goldensmith. And guess who was sitting there smoking a cigar as long as my arm? Musharraf. Ji haan. General Saab himself. Stuffed into a suit. Red tie. Diamond cuff lings. Bold as Brasso with white, white side burns and rest of head as jet black as my Ferragamo kay patent leather courts. Not looking itna sa bhi ashamed. I wanted to go up and tell him, while you are sitting here smoking cigars as long as my arm and dying your hair jet black and being looked after by MiFix, we are sarrhoing in 120 degrees heat in Lahore and that also without electricity, without water, with bombs bursting like phul jharees around us. And in case you didn't know, we are also in the middle of a huge economic slum, okay? And no offence, but I think so that's all your doing. Yours and that Short Cut Aziz's who I saw strolling down Slone Street yesterday as if it belonged to his own father. Janoo karoed Mush a dirty look, but not even this much effect it had on him. So besharam. Honestly!

Because I'm fair minded, and I don't want anyone to say that I don't give any lift to Oxford Street, I went to Selfridges sale also and bumped into whole of Pakistan's karobari community there in the ground floor only. Most of them were cueing outside the Channel and Looey Vitton ki sections and while they were waiting they were doing time pass by gossiping in lowered voices about each other, but only about those further down the line who couldn't hear. Vaisay I've noticed that way we desis are very considerate. We never do burai of people to their faces. Also went to SOS villages ki charity ka play organized by Dr Anwar's daughter Sammy—voh yahan hoti hai, na, in Kingstone—and met rest of Pakistan there too. Lubna Majeed was there, bhai, Izzat's wife, and Dr Ghazala Hameed and Anwar and Nazli Majeed and Meliha Zaman and so on and so fourth. Hai, this is what I love most about London. It's Lahore but with shops and electricity.

July 2010

Forty-two killed in bomb blast at shrine of Data Durbar
Butterfly wonders what bomb blasts in Lahore have to do with
her

I was enjoying so much in London, na, seeing films and going
to Royal China and Zooma and Harrods and Anna Bells and
hanging up with all my friends from Lahore and Isloo in
their flats in Kensington and enjoying London's nice soft heat
when suddenly the phone came and spoilt everything. It was
Mummy to say there'd been bombs in the shrine of Data Saab
in Lahore. Forty people had died and she didn't know how
many injured.

'Mummy,' I said, 'it's very sad and all but what does it have
to do with us?'

And then she said quietly, 'Jonkers was there.'

'*Jonkers?*' I yelled. 'Don't tell me something's happened to
him. Is he okay? What was he doing there?'

'No, he's not okay . . .'

Apparently poor Jonkers had gone to Data's to maano
a mannat, you know, make a wish. He hasn't been able to
find a new wife, na, and even though he's tried his bestest

94

to find a nice decent type, he's been alone since that gold dogger Miss Shumaila ran away taking his Honda salon and Aunty Pussy's hairloom yearrings. So he went to Data Sahib to ask for some help. He took five thou to distribute among the poors and he took his driver because parking is so hard there.

Anyways, Jonkers had just entered the saint's tomb area and because it was hot and so full of people and Jonkers is not used to heat and crushes, na, so he just gave sign to his driver that you go on and I'll follow. So the driver plunged into the crowds and Jonkers was coming slowly, slowly, every now and again stopping to wipe his sweaty face with his hanky, when suddenly there was an almighty bang and Jonkers couldn't remember anything afterwards. When the bomb burst, he was knocked off his feet and as he fell he hit his head on the side of some stone steps. And because he's bald the gash is very deep and he has also got con cushion and he stayed fainted for such a long time that Aunty Pussy thought he'd gone inside a comma.

Anyways, he's in the hospital with his head stitched up but his driver is dead. He was killed out write because it turned out he was standing quite close to the suicide bomber. The driver was twenty-eight years old and he had three children all under seven years old. His wife is twenty-five. His name was Naeem. He was Aunty Pussy's old driver, Saleem's, son. He used to wear leatherette jackets and he taught Kulchoo how to fly kites.

The night after the bombs burst we went to have dinner with Lahori friends, Bunty and Tara, who have a flat here on the backside of Selfridges only (four bed, four bath, costing at least three million quids) and when someone said, 'Oho very sad about the bomb in Lahore,' Bunty eik dum said, 'The Americans are behind it.' Normally it's Janoo who shouts when people say stuppid things like that but this time, I couldn't help myself.

'Yes, the two bombers were blonde blue-eyed baseball players, weren't they, From Canttucky?' I said. 'And before that, the guys who killed the Ahmadis in that mosque in Lahore, they were also Amreekans. Big, big blacks from Menhettan. It's never us, is it? It's always someone else.'

July 2010

General Kayani to stay on as army chief
Butterfly fears for Jonkers' sanity

We've come home from lovely London to bore Lahore and found two things. One, that rains are still here and still falling every day and, two, that General Kayani is also still here. Khair rains tau will pass away after two, three weeks but there's no hope of Kayani passing away any time soon. His three-year term was going to be up in October but instead of appointing a new army chief, the guvmunt's given him an extension, na.

Janoo is very depress. Ten years of Ayub, he says. Eleven of Zia. Eleven of Musharraf. Aur ub? But you know what, I've tau stopped asking. What's the point of khappaowing your brain for nothing? It's not as if *we* can do anything.

So anyways, instead of sitting at home and getting all depress with Janoo, I went to see Jonkers. He'd been hurt in the Data Durbar blast, na. He's come back from hospital and is now recooprating at home only. I found him in his lounge. He had a big fat bandage round his head and still looked shocked jaisa. So much weight he'd lost also. He was lying on his sofa with his striped flannel kay pyjamas hanging off him, so thin he's become.

'Hai, Jonkers,' I said, 'how've you lost so much of weight? Tell na. I also want to loose the pounds I've put on my hips from eating all those Zoo Ma kay dim sums.'

'Easy,' he said with a crooked sa smile. 'Just go to a congested public place and hang around till a bomb explodes. If you don't get blown to bits—which in fact will solve all your weight problems instantly—the smell of singed flesh and the sight of flying body parts and the sound of children's screams ringing in your head for weeks afterwards should do it.'

'Haw, Jonkers,' I said. 'What you are saying?'

And then he laughed in a weird sa way and said, 'Fasten your seat belt, Apa. We're in for the ride of our lives.' And then in a thin si voice, like a PIA air-hostess he chanted, 'Please take the flat bit of your seat belt and insert it . . .'

'I think so I should be going, Jonkers,' I said quickly. I got up to go and in my hurry I left behind my new Moo Moo ka bag, the one I got from Harrods. So he called out from my behind, 'Jaatay waqt apna dasti saaman lay jana mutt bhooliye. Hamaray saath suffer karnay ka bohat shukriya. Allah hafiz.'

August 2010

Worst floods in Pakistan's history: Fourteen million affected
Has someone done black magic on Pakistan, wonders Butterfly

I think so someone has done kaala jadoo on Pakistan. First earthquake, then Taliban in Swat, and now floods. One humanity crisis after another. And all on such big, big scales. Even that UN ka President, no sorry, Secretary General (vaisay aren't secretaries always women?) Banksy Moon was saying he'd never seen anything like it. And he should know because he himself comes from Thailand or China or some place like that where lots of rains come.

Vaisay every time I see the TV, I feel scared. All those miles and miles of water, I swear it's like Noah's Arch ka flood. It's like looking at pictures of a sea. For the first three days, Janoo just sat in front of the TV with his hands in his head. I mean head in his hands. Then when I said keh chalo, Janoo, let's give to guvmunt's appeal, he looked up and snarled, 'And have them pillage it? No thanks.'

I said, 'Phir kya karna hai? Khud ja keh dena hai?'

'Yes,' he said, 'we have to do it ourselves.'

So he called Mulloo, Tony, Sunny, Akbar, Baby and Tito

and said that I'm leaving for Kot Addu in two days time and you must all help me fill up a truck with bottled water, medicines, tents and food and I'll go and give to flood kay victims with my own hands only. And I must say everyone gave with open hearts. Because unlike guvmunt, Janoo has a good rep, na (even though he fights with everyone on politics, basically everyone trusts him and knows that he won't eat even a paisa of someone else's money). Kulchoo also went with him and he, shweetoo baby, gave fifteen thou from his saved up Eidees and birthday money and things. And Cuckoo Bhaijan—oho baba, of Fazal Din Chemist's only—gave the medicines free.

Anyways, it took Janoo four days to come back. And when they got back he and Kulchoo were so exhausted they couldn't speak even. So Janoo and I didn't fight for two full days. But now Janoo's got his speech back and in between telling everyone how terrible the sich really is, he rats and raves at the rest of the world for not helping Pakistan.

Apparently, when Hatty's earthquake came Britishers alone raised 110 million pounds for them. And for us they've given just seven millions. Dekho zara! Kanjooses! And after all the millions we've spent on buying their Burberry bags and their McQueen clothes, not to mansion the flats we've bought in London and that also in the nicest parts. Janoo says foreigners are not giving because they don't trust anyone in Pakistan— neither the useless thieving politicians nor this double dealing army which takes West ka paisa with one hand and paloes jihadis with the other. Meanwhiles our poors drown. Sooo unfair vaisay.

September 2010

Woman found dead in Mardan
Butterfly attends a school reunion

Last week I was invited to a reunification of my Convent ki class. It was a ladies' lunch at Punjab Club only. Pehlay tau I thought, bhai, kaun bother karay? In any case, most girls kay saath tau mein nay loose touch kar lee hai. I only see Ruby and Maha and that also once in a blue mood. Phir Maha called and said, 'Yaar chalte hain, dekhain tau sahi what has become of everybody. Ruby is also coming.' So being the soft obligating type—and also because my kitty lunch that day was cancelled, I said, 'Acchha baba, agar tum insist karti ho . . .'

Just between you, me and the four walls, when I was at school I was a little bit plumpish and I had frizzy hair and also my teeth were all crooked. And I also had a small spattering of pimples. So when I was getting ready that day I pulled out all the stocks. After all, they should know that what a sophisty swan I've become. So I put on my skinny Versace jeans which have rhino stones entrusted on the seems. And on top I wore my Maje ka green lace ka sleeveless top with no lining in the back. And I wore my green six-inch heel waali Jimmy Choo sandals. And emerald year studs and emerald bracelet and emerald ring. I told Ruby and Maha I'd meet them there only. And then I sat and waited and waited in my bedroom, till it was almost two and then I went. Bhai, fashionably late bhi tau hona hota hai, na.

Anyways, when I arrived I thought I'd come mistakenly to a ladies' dars—you know, religious meeting. Half the women were in hijab and there were also three or four ninjas—full black burka and niqab. All of them were fat and old. All of them were wearing flappy say bore shalwar kameezes in sober say colours, except the ninjas, who I don't know what they were wearing underneath their ninja outfits. All of them turned round to look at me when I came in. Nobody smiled, nobody said hello. Jahils!

Eventually this fat hijaban busybody, she waddled up to me and said, 'Maybe you are in wrong . . . Hai, is that you? Look everyone, it's her only. How much she's changed. Remember when she was so fat and pimply? And had that Afro? Look at her now. Dressed like a Bollywood extra from a club ka scene.'

'And haw, look at you,' I laughed. 'You are Bushra, na? Uff Allah, how much you have changed also! I remember you from when you were thin and pretty.'

At that her mouth squeezed up like a dried raisin and she hissed, 'You used to sit in the back of the class with all the other dumbos and fail in maths. *And* geography *and* Islamiyat. Once you even tried to do my cheating in a test. Cheater cock.'

'And you used to khisko from school with Tina Khan's brother. I remember once when your mother caught you on the back of his motorcycle. She pulled you off by your oily platts. Vaisay do you still have platts under that polyester tablecloth on your head?'

'For your info, it's a hijab and I wear it because I'm a proud and pious Muslim, okay? And you're going to hell and I'm going to heaven.'

'As long as I'm not going on the back of a Yamaha motorcycle, baba, I don't care where I end up.'

Then thanks God, Ruby and Maha, they came up and dragged me off to meet some others. And guess what? Three of them are already grandmothers. Zara imagine karo! And they look like grandmothers also, with flat shoes and chests like gao takias. The others were banging on about their children's rishtas, all arranged of course. And it was all mashallah this and inshallah that. And they'd all done five, five umras each and God knows how many Hajjs. And they meet every Friday for a one dish dars. Uff! You can't even imagine what I went through, yaar! Mulloo and all, they also talk about umras and I also keep my fasts but we're not like these losers.

I tell you there was not a single stilettoe in sight, not even one false eyelash, nor a single spaghetti strap to lift my mood. Hai, I thought to myself, what century is this, what planet? Mein kahaan phass gayee hoon? I swear it was like that TV programme from when I was a child, *Star Track*, in which their space ship sometimes landed on some planet where people looked zara say familiar but then they spoke strange, strange and behaved odd, odd.

Last draw was when lunch was served and I was about to put ketchup on my fries, and this woman, I think so her name was Uzma, she caught my arm and said, 'Yeh Heinz ka ketchup hai, don't eat this. It's made from pigs' bones!' I tau put my plate down there and then, and like Captain Kirk, who was in charge of the space ship in *Star Track*, I tau turned my own ship around and I zoomed out of there, and headed straight to Sunny's.

She was lounging in her lounge in a bubble gum pink Juicy Cotour tracksuit with her hair in curlers watching that cartoon type film, *Avatar*. As soon as I arrived, I told her what had happened and she laughed till she became historical.

'Uff, Sunny, bus bhi karo, it's not *that* funny,' I said. 'But you know what's really ajeeb? These girls, their mothers used to be so mod in the 70s. Remember how they all wore hipster saris and bell bottoms and Cleopatra eyeliner and just look at this lot now. I swear, what happened to them?'

'General Zia happened to them,' she yawned and then she ordered filtered coffee and finger sandwiches and mini kebabs with Heinz ketchup and for the next two hours, we gossiped about people's divorces, and their affairs and their scandals, and it was only then that I finally felt I'd come back to my own planet.

October 2010

CIA says Al-Qaeda in Pakistan hit hard in US attacks
Butterfly ponders admission criteria for schools

Last night I slept without my AC on full blast. That means, thanks God, that summers are going. And if summers are going, that means winters are coming. And if winters are coming then that means wedding and party season is also coming.

I told all this to Janoo yesterday and he said that I had astounding powers of seduction. Or was it reduction? Whatever. All I know is that he is impress with me. And so he should be! After all, I've been to Kinnaird College and Convent of Jesus and Mary. Koi mazaak nahin hai, okay? And this also, when only old family, khandani types used to get admission and not just any old upstarter. Nowdays tau ji anyone who is everyone can just walk in and be received like royalty. Just between you, me and the four walls, children of shopkeepers and chhota, chhota business types, like you know car work shops and shamiana wallahs, they are also getting in. So you can just imagine how much the standards have fallen.

Okay baba, the kids are little parhakoo types who get a hundred A stars in their exams and win cups at debates vaghera and also get into the top ki foreign ki universities like Yale and Princedon and LSC on full scholarships. But it's not as if you go to a school to do studies only, you know. You go to meet people—people who's brothers and sisters you will marry later, people with whom you will do kitty parties and GTs, and people who you will invite into your home and introduce to other people you know. I mean, studies tau is only a teeny tiny part of it.

You know, if I was to start a school—which I never will because I tau baba can't do all that bhaag dorh and work shirk—anyways, if I was to start a school, I would be least bothered about children's test results and things. I wouldn't have any of these stuppid jaisay admission tests of maths and reading writing shiting and all. I would do only one check up. That of bagground. Those with good baggrounds—children of sugar mill wallahs and big textile typhoons and other business magnets and of course, big, big landlords would get in straight away. Janoo, who was sitting there as I was telling this to Mulloo over the phone, asked me later, 'And where do you stand on children of generals and civil servants and politicians? Would they get into your exclusive school?'

Hmm, must say I'm a little bit double minded about that. As far as being khaata peeta is concerned, there's nobody as blessed as generals' kids and the kids of bureau cats and politicians. That tau is a well knowned fact. But are they khandanis? Well, if the politicians were landed feudals in the first place then tau they would get admission, I told Janoo.

But they would have to own at least five, six villages. I'm not giving admission to owners of only one square of land, okay?

'So your selective school is open to khandani chors? Reassuring to know. What about the rest?'

'I think so if they've had money for thirty years then their bagground becomes good. They become khandani.'

'So the generals who had their snouts in the trough during Zia's time, they're all twenty-four-carat khandani now?' asked Janoo. 'And the bureaucrats who stole fortunes in the '80s, also make the grade. But the slowcoaches who began robbing in earnest only in the '90s one must condemn. Is that right?'

'Bhai, I don't know,' I said. 'Why are you eating my head with such stuppid, stuppid questions?'

'Because you raised the subject . . .'

'I didn't raise anything, okay? All I'm saying is that wedding season is coming and my friend Paro of Paro's Perfect Parties is saying times are so bad that even well off khaata peetas, poor things, they are having to make do with just four functions worth six crores rather than six functions for nine crores. Honestly, it's so heart rendering. What, what else is this economic slum going to force on us?'

'I shudder to think,' said Janoo.

November 2010

Millions still homeless after floods
Butterfly plans a big party

Yesterday while me and Janoo were lounging in the lounge, I said to him, 'I think so, I should have a barha khaana. For seventy, eighty people. We could call a hundred also, mashallah, plenty of rooms in the lawn, but hundred zara over nahin ho jata? Mulloo will say we are show-offing. Anyways, eighty is a more reclusive number.'

'I don't think this is . . .'

'I think so we should have one table of desi food, one of western, and one of Chinese. And maybe one table of cheeses from Dubai. Frankly speaking, I tau can't stand the smell of those stinking running cheeses but looks impressive, na, and people will think hai yeh kitnay sophisty hain. And what else? Two tables of desert tau must hai. Both western and desi. Two types of music also. Both alive of course. One band of those kurta, surma types who can sit inside and play "Chalte chalte youhin koi mil gya tha" on harmonium and tabla and another group outside in pants and frilly shirts who can play "I will always love you" by Wintery Houston on the guitar and drums. Kitna stylish lagay ga, nahin?'

'I really don't feel . . .'

'I think so I'd better call J&S party planners tomorrow only and tell them to start thinking a nice si theme. How about "You Only Live Twice"? Or maybe, "Live and Let Die?" Haan? Are you listening, ji?'

'I am listening and I am appalled. At a time such as this, how can you even think of something so crass?'

'Haw. Kyoon? Koi mar gya hai?'

'Has it escaped your notice that over a million people are still homeless from the floods?'

'You know I've done my zakat,' I said. 'Gave two lakhs to the flood people. So I don't have a guilty conscious, thank you very much.'

'Are you not aware of how it will look? Our own chowkidar's entire village was swept away in Muzaffargarh. They're still living in tents. How do you think he'll feel when he sees your party with the bands and the food and the hundred people? Haan?'

'Look at you! What a hippo crit you are! Always telling Kulchoo that "Beta, do what you have to. If you worry about what people will say, you'll never get anything done in this world."'

'I give up. There's no point talking sense to the senseless. All I know is that I'm not paying for this vulgar party.'

'Vulgar ho gay tum! Vulgar ho gi tumhari maan. Vulgars hon gi tumhari sisters. Vulgar ho ga . . .' I was still speaking when he got up and left the room, slamming the door. Rude jaisa! I swear Janoo mein zara si bhi kissy kay liye koi feeling nahin hai . . .

December 2010

Trade deficit hits all-time high
Wedding season starts with a bang

Wedding season, mashallah-mashallah, has started with a bang. Hai, bhai where are you? With wedding of Prime Minister Gillani's son only. Full five day extravaganza it was. Must say our PM's so beloved that people have been falling over themselves to go to his functions. I said to Janoo, 'Hai, look how lucky he is. I didn't know that he had so many lovers.'

Janoo's lips switched and he said, 'No, neither did I. Lucky man. I wonder how he keeps his lovers so ardent?'

'Must be his charms only,' I said.

'That and a few other incentives. He makes poor old AZ look positively modest in his rakings.'

Aik tau when Janoo starts speaking you need a pictionary to understand him. Such big, big words and weird, weird sentences he uses. Only I could have done guzara with someone like that, who's never been able to forget his Oxford ki education.

But thanks God he's speaking to me at least. Two, three

days ago when that jhooti khabar about Abida Parveen's death came, he tau straight away sank into the deepest bloom. As you know, at best of times, he's a zinda laash but I swear this time tau he became so depress, so depress that I thought bus, now his nerves are shattered.

But chalo, thanks God, news came that Abida was okay and then Janoo started being a bit more normal again. Or as normal as he can be.

I think so I'll go off to Dubai for a bit. Maybe in Muharram only. Zara sa change ho jaye ga. One needs a change, na. To become fresh. Varna one becomes stale. Like yesterday's rotis. All hard, hard, cold, cold. The only problem is I have to tell Janoo. Will have to find the right mauka. I think so I'll go and buy him a nice CD of Abida Parveen and when he's listening and is all carried off by the music, then I'll ask him in my softest, nicest voice, 'Janoo, mein chaar din ke liye Dubai na ho aaoon?'

December 2010

Pakistani role is suspected in revealing US spy's name
Jonkers and Butterfly meet a psychotherapist

Jonkers wants to have an acchha sa dinner for about thirty friends at his house but bechara kya karay? Being a shy, shareef type bachelor he doesn't know how to throw one and he doesn't want to ask Aunty Pussy because she'll give him a cheap sa, cut price type event because you know, na, what a kanjoos makhi choos she is. So he came to ask me because he knows that I am dinner lady of Lahore. I tau told him saaf, saaf. I said, 'Jonkers, I'd happily have done all the intezaam for you myself only, but what to do, yaar? I'm so busy because it's the wedding season, na. But let's do like this: let me take you to a party planner who'll do a real classy khaana for you.'

'I'm happy to pay, Apa,' he said, 'but I don't want anything brash, if you know what I mean.'

'Haw, Jonkers,' I said. 'Me and brash? My tau angels don't even know meaning of brash. Don't worry, leave it to me, I'll take you to a theek thaak person.'

Vaisay tau I would have gone to my friend Paro of Paro's Perfect Parties but on deflection, I think so she's not right for

Jonkers. She's all big, big bows and soft peach lightening and her food is all nibbles and dribbles and her sound track is always 'I will always love you-hoo-hoo' type moody numbers. I think so if Paro does Jonky's khaana all his friends will think keh he's a homo.

So instead I took him to Neeli, of Bonanza Bashes. One Halloween party she did a Haath of Darkness theme, with bloody hand prints all over the walls and lightening was all dark, dark, scary, scary and there were white tablecloths with big dhabbas of tomato ketchup which looked just like blood and sound track was all howls and screams. I think so she'll be more up his sweet.

But when we turned up at her office, I couldn't see that big red and yellow board of Bonanza Bashes. Okay, I hadn't been there since last year but still I was sure keh jagah tau vohi hai. And then I saw a chhota sa, sober sa sign saying Dr Neelum Qayyum. So with Jonkers in toe, I went inside and jahaan pehlay there was this fat man, Akhoo, in slippers and creased shulloo kurta who used to do all her lightening and sounds vaghera, now there was this Miss Shumaila type secretary with tight shirt and tight hair behind a desk.

'Aap ka Dr Qayyum kay saath time hai?' she asked, smiling tightly.

'Er, actually, er . . .' stammered Jonkers.

'Ji haan,' I said and, grabbing Jonkers by the hand, I swept passed her and went straight away inside.

Inside office was same to same except that where last year there were big, big photos of her old parties, now there were washed up prints of misty land escapes and instead of the yellow walls and orange curtains, it was all beige, beige, bore, bore.

Neeli's desk was against the wall like before only but Neeli herself was definitely not like before only. The old Neeli used to wear polyester jungle prints and had long shaggy hair streaked orange and golden and she wore more chains than the Prisoner of Zenda. New Neeli's hair was dark and scrapped back into a tight sa bun and she had steal brimmed glasses and halki si lip gloss and plain mouse colour cotton ka suit. Bus. Aur haan, oopar, a doctor's waala white coat.

'Haw, Neeli,' I said, 'tujhay kya hua hai? I mean, what happened to Bonanza Bashes?'

She said, 'Bus yaar, bohat ho gya tha. You know when I became an event manager tau only nice people from nice homes were in this business. Now every light wallah and every kursi wallah has become a party planner. Always undercutting everything you do. It's become a very ganda crowd. Hardly anyone can speak any English. So I thought, chalo Neeli, kuch aur kartay hain. First I thought I'd open a beauty saloon. But uff! The thought of training all the waxing waalis and the facials waalis and rollers waali and constantly dealing with "Baji, meri burrday hai thousand rupees ka udhaar day dain" and "Baji, meray bhai ko job day dain, pliss", it was too much for my nerves, yaar. So I thought keh koi esa kaam karoon that I can do just by myself only.

'And then one day I came across this add in some magazine which said that just with a two week ka course you can become a fully pledged life coach cum psychotherapist and start fixing patients and all. And you can charge fees of ten, ten thou for an hour. So then I thought bhai, why not? Tau I went off to Singapur and there I did the course, two hours a day for two weeks—aagay peechay I did time pass by seeing films and doing shopping. And bus, I came back, took off the old sign, painted the office, had this coat made and lo, Dr Qayyum aap kay saamnay hain.'

'When did you start?' I asked.

'Bus, yehi koi four months ago.'

'And you already have patients?'

'Tau aur?'

'Like who?' I asked.

'Apa, I really don't think it's any of our . . .' started Jonkers.

'Bhai, first tau there's Champa Feroze, you know her, na?' said Neeli, doing total ignore of Jonkers.

'You mean Champa the chor?' I laughed.

'Apa, that's no way to speak . . .'

'She's actually a klepto, picks up just anything,' said Neeli. 'Help nahin kar sakti, na. Anyways, she came to me because she was leaving a big barbecue party and they were standing by the front door with three other couples doing thanks shanks to their hosts, when Champa leaned forward to kiss her hostess goodbye, lost her footing on the polished marble stairs and her clutch bag slipped out of her hands, fell with a thud on the floor and flew open, and out rolled four seekh kebabs and a bottle of Tobasco. In front of everyone.'

'Haw, so how did you cure her?'

'Apa, please this is none of our business . . .'

'Shush, Jonky, don't be bore. Haan, so tell na, Neeli.'

'Bhai, first tau I said that jub aap baahar jaati hain, please stomach full kar kay jaya karein. And two, meherbani say don't ever carry a handbag or wear clothes with pockets, okay?'

'Haw, tau theek ho gayee?'

'Kabhi kabhi she still sneaks things into her bra, but chhoti, chhoti cheezain, a coffee spoon here, a chaabi there . . .'

'Hai, how funny. Tell more, na.'

'Apa, please!' begged Jonky, but we both ignored him.

'Aik barha successful businessman hai,' Neeli continued, 'Jawad Salam, fat, middle-aged, with big frizzy fundo type beard, has six children, two grandchildren. And guess what he has?'

'What?'

'A weakness for stilettoe heels and crimson lipstick.'

'Tau what's wrong with that? Jonky also likes high heels, kyoon, Jonky?'

'For himself?'

'Haw, Mr Salam khud pehenta hai?'

'Really, Dr Qayyum, I insist that you must stop immediately,' said Jonky, getting up. 'This is very unethical. You must respect your patients' confidentiality.'

'Hai, tau mein nay kya kaha hai?' said Neeli.

January 2011

Salman Taseer, governor of Punjab, gunned down by bodyguard
Butterfly attends his funeral

Three days ago our friend Salman Taseer was murdered. He was shot ten times by a bearded bodyguard as he was coming out of a restaurant in Isloo at lunch time. The other bodyguards, they just stood and watched. When his killer was taken to jail, lawyers showered him with rose petals and put garlands around his neck, like you do to those returning from Hajj. They think so he's a hero because he killed a man who said that the blasphemy law is unfair because it targets the poors.

So this poor Christian woman, Asya Bibi, she was accused of blasphemy because she had a fight with some Muslim women and they said that they heard her saying bad things about Islam. And you know, na, that the punishment for blasphemy is death? And so they immediately slapped blasphemy on her and she was taken to jail and there Salman went to visit her and to basically show that she wasn't alone, na. And he also came on TV and said that this is not being right. We shouldn't

117

be like this and when mullahs asked him to take back what he'd said, he said no I stand by what I said. So all the fundo types, they went up in smokes. And next thing we know, he's been gunned down.

Me and Janoo, we went to his funeral. It was small. And you know what? Hardly anybody big from his party, PPP, was there. And they couldn't find a mullah to lead the funeral prayer because even if they didn't think he was a villain they were scared that what if they also get gunned down? And Salman was the guvnur of Punjab, you know. And when he was alive everyone wanted to go to his parties and be his friend and get their works done by him. Aur ub . . .

But you know what is really, really sub say worst? That even friends of ours whose kids are in college in the US and who serve drink in their home and would sell their grandmothers for a green card, even they are saying that he wasn't a good Muslim because he was too westernized and he said no to the blasphemy law and so basically he got what he deserved. I mean fundos say tau mein expect karti thi, but for God's sake yaar, these people are like us only, we have uthna bethna with them, they come to our house for dinners and all.

These days, you know, I feel like I'm living in a horror film. You know the ones where zombies or alients have been chasing you through a big black forest and you're scared and you're running and running and your legs are heavy and your chest is bursting and your breath is coming all fast, fast and then suddenly you see the lights of your house up ahead and with the last of your breaths you run to your house and rench open the door and slam it shut behind you. And upstairs you can hear your brothers and sisters talking and arguing and in the kitchen your mother is cooking and so you stagger into the kitchen and collapse into a chair. And she's standing at the choola stirring something and she doesn't turn around and you gasp and you say, 'Oh Mother, you don't know what happened to me . . .' And she says quietly, 'What happened?' And then she turns around and you see that she has also become a zombie with crazed eyes and blood dripping from her mouth. And you realize that your home is not your home and that your mother is not your mother and that you are safe nowhere. I feel just like I'm in that film . . .

February 2011

Turmoil in Egypt, as anti-Mubarak protest gathers strength
Butterfly laments the banning of basant

I'm down in the dumbs. Everything seems so dark and bloomy after Salman's murder. Every day we see pictures of that beardo weirdo who shot Salman and you know what? People are sending mithai to his house and offering his family their cars and bags of money and whatnot because they think he's a soldier of Islam. And obviously guvmunt can't hang him because there'd be riots on the streets. So he's sitting like a VIP in jail while Salman lies in his grave.

Chalo, let's talk of something less depressing. This time of year normally I'd be getting all excited about basant and the parties sharties that happened for it. But of course, they've gone and band basant, na. By 'they' obviously I mean the guvmunt. But guvmunt hasn't done it all on its own. No, no, it would never have the guts. They've done it under pressure from mullahs, na. Because as you know, mullahs can't stand the sight of anyone having fun, being the killed joys that they are.

So what they've done is that they've pretended that the

ban is for our own goods only. Because dors, kite threads and all, are very dangerous, na, and they cut people's hands and throats also and on top of that, when chasing kites lots of young bacchas fall from roofs and high walls and things and kill themselves. And so for our own well fear they've gone and band basant.

But what I'm thinking is this: if they were so concerned about our well fear and so keen to keep us all safe and found, I wonder why they don't ban guns and bombs and pistols shistols, haan? Those tau you can buy in the market as easily as buying chapattis and every aera vaghera nathoo khaira has at least two, two Kalashnicoughs. Why they are not banning those? And also, why they are not banning all these religious outfits like the various Lashkars and Jaishes and whatnots which go around slitting people's throats? Haan? Why only dors and kites? Bloody hippo crits.

March 2011

Bangladesh stages impressive opening ceremony for cricket World Cup
Why were no fatwas passed against the organizers, asks Butterfly

Haw, look at the Bangladeshis! Look how quietly, quietly they've gone and put on such a tabahi show for the cricket world cup ki opening ceremony. All that music and singing and dancing and zabardast stadiums and electronic kites and those tall, tall buildings and fire works and whatnot. And I swear, not a single bomb exploded during it—even though girls were singing and dancing on the stage side by side with men. No one came in and sprayed all the dancers and the watchers with bullets from Kalashnicoughs. And I think so no fatwas even were passed against the dancers saying that their marriages were from now on illegal and that they were living in sins with their husbands and therefore illegible for stoning by death for adultery. Aur tau aur, no one's ambushed and attacked the players even. Imagine!

I know the Bangladeshis are Muslims but maybe they don't have enough of izzat and ghairat and all, you know, like we do. Because if they had, they would have immediately shot all the girl dancers for spoiling their honour and bringing shame on them and burst a bomb under the Prime Minister for sitting there and smiling and enjoying in her sari and bun. And they would have threated all the people who bought tickets to the ceremony that if you go to watch this display of western type fahaashi we will break your legs. In fact, they would have called a huge hartaal up and down the country and made sure that no one went. And next day huge, huge professions of a million bearded men would have come out on to streets and said, 'We won't stand for this western influence' and for days afterwards on TV there would have been long discussions about how we are trying to become the pet animals of the West and how we are in danger of loosing our precious identity and how this is a plot against us and how the whole world is out to get us and guests would have come and said we have become beghairat. And Imran Khan would have said that we are brown sahibs and have become westoxified. None of that happened in Bangladesh so I guess they couldn't be having too much of izzat and ghairat and all.

Vaisay it would have been nice if we'd been allowed to host a couple of matches also, in Isloo and Lahore and Karachi. All the countries of South Asia are doing, except us. Only we have not been allowed. I said this to Janoo and he snorted and said, 'After what happened to the poor Sri Lankan cricketers, who were the only team kind enough to come and play here, do you think any foreign team wants to come here now? Better get used to this isolation. There's going to be a lot more of it.'

Aik tau Janoo is always such a ray of sunshine, na.

April 2011

On second day of CNG strike, ministry feels the heat
Butterfly and Aunty Pussy squabble over a 'hairloom' necklace

Me and Aunty Pussy, we're not talking. We've had a bit of a tiff, a small sa jhagra, na. It was over her diamond and emerald choker. You know, na, that she always said she'd give it to me? Because after Jonkers' short but disastrous marriage to that cheapster chor, Miss Shumaila, she can't trust Jonkers to find a daughter-in-law worthy of inheriting her necklace. Well, yesterday we'd gone to her house and Kulchoo had taken her some special diabetic chocolates that he'd seen in Al Fatah's. (You are knowing, na, that Aunty Pussy has sugar? Anyways, she has.) So you can imagine her reaction.

'Hai, my Kulchoo, my baccha, light of my eyes, piece of my liver, slice of my heart. You've gone so much on me: loving, giving, considerate, generous, thoughtful. Not like *some* people I could mention.' And then she gave me a sarrhial look. You know, eyes slitted, mouth pursed up like a dried plumb, chin like pitted stone. And why? Because I'd refused to send her my maid to die her hair. 'Stop being kanjoos, Aunty, and go to the hairdresser,' I'd said to her. You know, na, that she uses Kala Koala and that also number 001, jet black. Her head looks like a crow's backside. And anyways, my maid was busy shrinking the thirty voile pieces I've bought for my summers ki wardrope. Daily wears only. For evenings, I think so I'll get organdie and lace. So natch, I couldn't spear her to die Aunty Pussy's hair. So when Kulchoo gave Aunty Pussy the chockies, she gave a real sly sa smile and murmured to him, 'When you get married, my moon, I'll give my emerald and diamond choker to your wife.'

'I don't want to prickle your balloon, Aunty Pussy, but by the time Kulch gets married,' I said, 'you'll be dead.'

'Why should I be dead? I'm only sixty-five. If Kulchoo gets married in fifteen years, I'll be eighty. And eighty is no age these days. Look at the Queen. Look at Clint Eastwood. Look at Nelson Medallion.'

'Don't mind, Aunty Pussy, but you're not sixty-five. You're seventy-four, okay?'

'Seventy-four ho gi tumhari maan!'

'Mummy's five years younger than you. Even I know that much.'

'Your mother is a liar.'

'Haw, Aunty Pussy, I don't think so you should say such bad things about Mummy. And that also in front of her grandson.'

'I'll say what I like and I'll do what I like. I'll wear my choker myself!'

'No offence, Aunty Pussy, but on your leathery old neck it will look ajeeb. You know, na, boorhi ghorhi laal lagaam?'

'For your information I have the neck of a swan. Even

that artist Bevan Pittman said so,' she yelled, her eyes blazing, hands shaking. 'And let me tell you ji, he painted only the most beautiful society ladies.'

Then I thought, what if she gets heart attack or something even worst? So I quickly calmed her down.

'Sure, Aunty, sure. You have the neck of a swan. An eldery, stuffed swan.'

After that she stopped talking to me. And now she's skulking. Aik tau she's become so touchy. Honestly. Why must I be surrounded only by touchy feely people?

May 2011

US Seals find Bin Laden in Abbotabad
Butterfly suspects her one-eyed tailor is Mullah Omar in disguise

Vaisay I'm so disappointed, so disappointed that don't even ask. Janoo used to say the only two institutions that have survived in Pakistan are the army and the family. So thanks God my family is very much all there, because after Osama was stolen in broad midnight from right under the army's noses by Americans and their seals (vaisay why did the soldiers bring seals with them? Funny animal to bring, no?), I don't think so I can say same for the faujis. Janoo of course is jumping up and down as usuals.

He says if OBL was living in the army's backyard all these years without the faujis having kaan-o-kaan ki khabar then they were criminally incontinent, sorry, sorry, I meant incompetent, and if they *did* know and were hiding him jaan kay then they're just plain criminal. But one thing I don't understand. If as Janoo says that for sixty years they've been drinking our blood and eating the country, not to mention all those billions also that they've khaowed from the Americans and instead of letting us build hospitals and schools and roads and gyms and beauty saloons and things they've been ordering fighter jets from arms catalogues and sumbarines and big bad bombs and radars and bullet proofed Mercs, and how come they can't even catch two helicopters, haan? Honestly! Incontinent or what?

And also all those stuppids like Imran Khan who wanted to go and do dharna in tribal areas to stop Americans flying drawns into Pakistan, bhai, you go and do your dharna in Rawalpindi because it's the generals who've given Americans permission to fly drawns into Pakistan. The poor guvmunt is tau so weak, so weak it can't even give orders for a kite to fly over Rawalpindi.

And also what does Imran mean, the war on terror is finished now. Haan? God knows who, who else is hiding in Pakistan? Maybe my jeweller is a RAW agent, who brings all his rubies shubies from Jaipur only. Maybe Ayman Al Johari is selling pistachios at a dry fruit stall in Liberty Market. Maybe Mullah Omar is working at my darzi's in Defence. Vaisay my darzi's new assistant has a big beard *and* he's blind in one eye. Maybe I should get a new darzi. Hai, but he gives such a good fitting . . .

May 2011

Hakim Ali Zardari passes away
Butterfly's friends split over whether or not to go to the funeral

Exactly half our friends are going to Nawabshah. Some have even chattered planes. For President Asif Zardari's father's funeral, baba, what else? Aur Nawabshah mein kya rakha hai? It's hardly as if it's a tourist destination like Bali or Istambull. So these friends are going to do afsos personally—I think so to suck up to the President—because people remember, na, who, who came at such occasions and who, who didn't.

The other half of our friends are staying puts. They're saying, 'Bhai, zaroor jaatay, but it's so hot' or that 'We tau would've gone jhutt say but what to do, we're going to London tomorrow.' I think so these second types are not sure that Asif Zardari is going to win the next election and they want to keep their options open, na. Being seen as a particularly close friend of Asif's might black fire, particularly if the new man is anti-Asif. Janoo says they're hedging their butts, whatever that may mean. Aik tau Janoo and his Oxen ki English!

Meanwhiles we are going nowhere. Not to Nawabshah, not to London, not to Singapore, not to Dubai. And why?

Because Janoo says he can't afford. I say baba, for God's sake sell some land and send the money out like all our friends are doing. Sunny and hubby tau have sold their back lawn even and sent the money to Koala Lumpure. They have a big house there, na. On Maha Teer's backside only. And Baby has that apartment in Missy Saga in Torontoe. And Fluffy and Aslam, they have that flat in London. Apparently Musharraf is their neighbour. But I think so they want to move soon because they're worried that if a Brit Asian jihadi targets Mush, he might get them by mistake. I've told Janoo that if you don't send some money out soon, I'm tau taking Kulchoo and leaving, even if I have to beg, borrow or scream. He says he can't sell the land of his great grand fathers. I said why you have to be last ghairat mand, haan? Take a sheaf from Imran Khan's book. See how he gets his kids educated abroad while telling us all to stay puts and give desi education to our children, has holidays in London while telling us all to sit and sarrho in bore Lahore, tells us to hate Amreeka then goes to raise money for his hospital over there, why you can't be like that, haan?

Journalist Saleem Shehzad's tortured body fished out of canal:
ISI denies murder
Butterfly gets a migraine

Uff, it's so hot, so hot, in Lahore it's like Gobby desert. My
air-conditioner pants like a dog who's run the marathong.
The water in the taps—even the cold taps—is hot. Even
while I'm showering, I'm sweating. People have heated pools
in places like Swizzerland and all, we should get cooled pools
in Lahore. Bhai, why not? Otherwise tau while you're doing
breast stroke you feel like you're being boiled alive in a giant
deg. I tau try not going outside in the day, but if I have to for
some majboori like a kitty party or something, the sun hits
me like a giant hammer on my head. I swear I've had four my
grains already this month. Each time, for two, two days I had
to lie in my bedroom with the pardahs drawn and whooshy
si, watery si music playing on my bedside.

That tape was part of a psychopath ilaj (or was it
naturopath? Khair, whatever) that Maha made me do. She
said that every time I take a painkiller I'm getting addicted to
it and if I carry on like this, in two years time I'd end up just

131

like Michael Jackson. 'You mean I'll become a world famous mega pop star?' I asked. No, she said, it meant I'd be dead of an overdouse of subscription pills. And then she offered to do a drug free ilaj for me for the tiny sum of ten thou, which she said was all the rage in Germany and Swizzerland vaghera. So she gave me this music which she said is from some place called Born (in Germany) only. She said it's the latest ilaj over there of everything from childbirth pains to heart pains. Apparently, no one takes medicines anymore in Born, not even after open heart surgery. Instead everyone just listens to 'celestial music' and does chanting shanting and bus, you're bright as rain in two minutes flat.

So this tape (Rs 3000), it was supposed to take me inside a trance and make me forget all about my headache. She also gave me some pink and blue coloured jhoota stones (Rs 3500), all pointy and jagged like Mulloo's teeth, and said that if I was to hold these crystals tightly in my mutthi I'd feel a deep calm stealing over me. And also she said to alight a donkey brown candle (Rs 3500) that's supposed to give off 'positive energy' when inhaled deeply.

Well, I'm sorry to say that I was neither put inside a trance nor did I feel anything steal over me, except a strong desire to do ultee. I tell you the watery music made me so sick, I felt like I was in a boat rocking back and fourth, fourth and back. And the 'crystals' (between you and me and the four walls, I think so they were plastic, made in China only) dug into my palm and also gave me sharp stabbing hand pain as well as my grain. And the candle I had to blow out after two minutes only because it gave off more black smoke than a rubber tyre

132

ki factory and it made me cough till I felt my kidneys were about to pop into my mouth.

So anyways, when Janoo came home from his evening swim and found me lying coughing and choking inside a darkened smoky room, he immediately gave me two tablets of New Rofen Express and opened the windows, and then he gently massaged my head and neck with Tiger Palm and in ten minutes flat, I promise by God, I was inside a trance. Then he left me to sleep and when I woke up he took me out for dinner to Cuckoo's Nest and he bought me jasmine bracelets on the way and we sat outside on the roof top of the restaurant and watched Badshahi Mosque all lit up like I Fell Tower, and I don't know from where it came (must be from Kashmir only, like all the best shahtooshes) but suddenly there was this cool si delicious si breeze (and no mosquitoes because, thanks God, they've all died in the heat) and as I sat there in the breeze and sipped ice cold badaam ka sherbet and sniffed my jasmine bracelets, I thought to myself, you know this garmi, I can cope up with it as long as I have Janoo . . .

Budget unlikely to prop up ailing economy
Butterfly jealous of wealthy Indian shoppers

Haw, didn't you know? I tau have been in London for two weeks now. Got here just on the day before the Harrods ki sale. Vaisay between you and me, walking into Harrods is like landing in Delhi airport—so many Indians, so many Indians that don't even ask. Saw this Indian girl with tight white jeans with visible panty line holding up a Prada ka bag to her bald pot bellied husband and saying, 'Kitna cute chhay, no?' Cheapster jaisi.

Janoo and Kulchoo are here also. We've rented a two bed compartment on the backside of Selfridges. Maid comes and cleans thrice a week but majaal hai keh she serves me tea in bed! Honestly, these British servants are so spoilt. Talking of servants, Janoo is very worried about his pheasants back in Sharkpur. Apparently there've been early rains in our absent. And the pheasants—oho baba, all the poors who live in his village—they're worried because their maize crop is lying in the open and getting all soggy and wet. I wanted to say to Janoo that it's their fault then for leaving it in the open. They should've brought it inside. But you know, na, that arguing with Janoo is total time waste. Janoo is also worried about floods again this year. Why he's worried I don't know. Because we tau mashallah say are in London.

What else to tell? Haan, went to Abid Imam's engagement party to Farah Parvez (she's daughter of Sir Anwar Parvez, na—very big businessman here). It was at the Doorchester only. Sitting down dinner for one hundred and twenty guests in the Orchid Room. Very tastily done and bride and groom looked very happy and the guests also looked very happy because food was very nice and company was also very nice and there was kathak performance afterwards. Also went to APWA's dinner to celebrate Pakistani women. Sherry Rehman, Amna Taseer, Sharmine Chinoy were there, Maheen Khan—looking stunning in steal grey satin jora with her short say steal grey hair—was there and General Musharraf with his jet black hair was also there. I don't know why he was there because he isn't a woman, you know. Anyways, he announced that he was going to give APWA 5000 pounds from his own pocket. As if we all give from someone else's pocket. But maybe being a general he doesn't know difference between his own pocket and his countrymen's pocket.

August 2011

Record rain sinks Lahore
Butterfly names her chauffeur's baby daughter

I've told you before also, na, that these days I'm in London. Well, I'm enjoying and everything except that news from home is not so good. Mulloo called and said that Sunny, who only went back from London two weeks ago, has told all the girls in our kitty group in Lahore that I should be thrown out, because I've been in London for so long now and who knows when I'll be back and really it's not fair on everyone else who shows up every month and gives their ten thou properly like shareef peoples. Dekho zara, snake of sleeve, back stabber jaisi. I know why she's being like this. Because she is jay—oho baba, jealous.

She is jay because she also wanted to stay on longer in London like me but they only had that compartment in Nell Grin House for three weeks and she was desperate because the PM's wife was visiting then and was doing a big khaana and Sunny wanted so much to go to that khaana and have her photos taken with the PM's wife (bechari, she's such a wanna bee) but their rental was finishing and you know, na, that London is so full to the grim with Arabs and Indians and Russians and even rich, rich Africans in high season that I swear the day your flat runs out, you're out on the street in two seconds. All the flats, all the houses, all the hotels, everything is so much full.

So anyways, she dropped fat, fat hints that we should empty out our kiraya ka flat for her and go back home because we've been here so long and all, but I thought who is she to ask, haan? Is this her father's flat? So I also did total ignore and when her date came and she had to leave, she gave me lots of sarrhial looks and made lots of sarrhial comments like, 'Bhai, you all tau have become pukka foreigners now. Your blood has turned white. And we, we tau are patriots, na, returning home to our own country because east or west, home is best,' and so on and so fourth. But I ignore karoed. Next I hear she's done a coo in the kitty against me. I swear, look at her!

And then our bearer, Raheem, calls from home and says there's been a big rain and our wall outside has fallen down and now anyone can walk into our garden from the street and I told Janoo and Janoo said we should ask Sunny's husband, Akbar Khan, to fix it because he has construction business and he can send his men around in three seconds flat and we can pay him when we get back and I said, 'Over my dead body, ji.' So I told Raheem to get some mazdoor types from the bazaar only and get it fixed and then Raheem said there was good news also. Miskeen the driver has had a baby girl and he and his wife want me to name her.

'What's she like?' I asked Raheem.

'Like her mother,' he said, 'fat, black and bad tempered.'

'Oh, in that case, I have the perfect name for her. Name her Sultana Rabia Khan.'

That's Sunny's real name.

Shahbaz Taseer, son of slain governor of Punjab, kidnapped
Butterfly's delight in returning home to Pakistan short-lived

I've come home to Lahore after three full months. Oho baba I was away, na. In London only. Had such a fab time going to cinemas, street walking, park strolling—total heaven. Na koi worry of abduction, na of kidnapping, na of hold-up at gun point. Kulchoo used to go out with friends at night, and that also on pubic transport, and I swear I never worried for one second even. Banda jaa kay total relax ho jaata hai. You only realize then in how much of tension you live over here. Of course, there was that little bit of rioting in London—and between you and me, it was quite scary with all those kaala goondas in hoodies roaming around—but then the guvmunt gave them all a good danda and it was back to normal in one week flat.

But respite of that in the end I was missing home so much, so much that don't even ask.

I wanted to see Mummy, wake up in my own bed in my own room, wanted to meet all my friends and hear all their gup shup and see what, what they'd done to their houses while

I've been away, go buy paan and flowers from Main Market and new lawn prints from Liberty Market, eat aloo gosht with proper tandoor ki roti (salad shalads are fine for a while but nothing like your own khaana, baba), watch desi TV cereals and new, new Indian films in my lounge while getting oil massage done to my head.

Haan so bus I've been back ten days and already I'm so tired and depress keh don't even ask. While I've been away apparently hundreds of people have been killed in Karachi. Shahbaz Taseer, Salman's son, has been kidnapped in broad daytime. Poor things, his mother and his young wife. No one knows where they have taken him.

Bijli is still not coming. And despite of it not coming the bijli ka bill is huge. The servants have eaten three boris of atta and one of sugar and six large tins of ghee (five kilos each) and I don't know how many maunds of meat and sabzis. Our backside wall fell in the rains and next door neighbour had a big robbery in the middle of Ramzan. They lost their TV, DVD, computers, mobiles, cash, jewellery, silver and their car. But they are so happy that the robbers didn't rape their daughter and kidnap their son that tomorrow they are doing big shukraanay ka khatam. Also it is still very hot. But I don't think so I'm allowed to say in case I'm taken to be anti-Pakistan, American/Indian/Israeli lover.

October 2011

Steve Jobs dies
Kulchoo becomes a twit

Kulchoo is a twit. He's mashallah say now fifteen and all day, all night he twits on the computer. Haw, don't you know what twitting is? No baba, it's not like knitting. Twitting is when you send short say messages about this and that to other twits and they read them and give replies. Like if you are about to gobble a chicken tikka at Barbecue Tonight, you twit that you are at Barbecue Tonight and about to gobble a chicken tikka and someone twits back to say that haw, lucky you, wish I was there also! A little bit like email but with whole world at same time.

So a few days back Kulchoo appeared in my room with a face longer than my arm.

'Hai, shweetoo, why are you looking so depress?' I asked him.

'I just read on Twitter that Steve Jobs is dead,' he said.

'Haw hai. Sorry, na. Who's he?'

'No one you'd know.'

'What do you mean "no one I'd know"? Haan? For

your information, I know all of Lahore, all of Isloo, half of Karachi, half of Dubai and a good spattering of Delhi also, okay?'

'That's why you won't know Steve Jobs.'

'Hai, Kulchoo, don't be like that. Tell na. Who was he? Anyone I should invite to my next khaana? Anyone important?'

'Only the founder of Apple and the man behind the Mac, the iPod, the iPhone and the iPad and Pixar.'

'Oh, bore. No one important then.'

What stuppid Kulchoo didn't tell me about Sleeve Jobs was that he was very rich also. Trust him to leave out the most important thing. Apparently he owned a big piece of Disney. And a computer company also. I think so it must be Facebook. Or Goggle. And I also found out that his father abandoned him when he was a baby. Men, I tell you! You can't even trust them this much. Honestly, vaisay his father must have smacked his forehead a thousand, thousand times afterwards, that oh ho, what have I done? A bit like Obama's father, no? If both these fathers had known who their sons would become, I bet you a million rupees—no, dollars, rupee tau is worth two paisas now—they would have kept them clamped in their arm pits. Chalo, as Mother Rosario at my Convent used to say, you read what you sew.

Talking of reading and sewing, Janoo says Pakistan's economic halaats are going from bad to worst. Apparently we have highest food inflation in hole of Asia. 'You're telling me?' I said. 'Thousand rupee note has become like hundred.

You go to Al Fatah and you buy one cheese, one bottle of olive oil and one packet of foreign ka butter and lo, your wallet is empty. Allah jaanay how the poors manage. Just as well they don't like olive oil and imported cheeses.'

November 2011

Imran Khan stages giant rally in Lahore
Butterfly feels a deep connection with Imran Khan

Bhai, I'm tau very impress. With what? Haw, where've you been? In Greens Land? I'm impress with Imran's rally in Manto Park, baba, what else? Auf taubah, you should have been there. There was so much of gaana bajaana and so much of nice, nice talk that made me so proud to be Pakistani. I think so there were at least a crore of people there. And thanks God, lots of PLUs also—People Like Us. You know, khaata peeta, English medium types who normally never come to political rallies. I mean I went, Mulloo went, Baby went, Sunny went. Even Aunty Pussy and Mummy went— imagine, at their elderly ages! Imran's woken us up like an alarmed clock, you know, because we are so much disgusted with status coup and so much hungry for change.

But then it's not surprising we all of us went to his rally, because between you, me and the four walls, Imran is also a PLU, na. I mean, if you think about it, he and I have quite a lot in commons. Like me he also goes regularly to London (he was there just now only, promoting himself and his book about himself, so goras will have to buy it). He has a nice house in Isloo, I have one in Lahore, all my bestest friends are PLUs and all his jigri yaars are also PLUs. He says his prayers and keeps rozas and gives qurbani and also goes to parties and so do I. He wears shulloo kurta here and western in London and so do I. He speaks Urdu and English and so do I. Only difference is, he reads Iqbal primers and I read *Good Times*.

Imran will give us full time bijli, he will do sullah with the Baloch and dig up their coals and give them to us Punjabis, he will do sullah with the Taliban so they will aik dum drop their weapons and become all lovey dovey with us, he will collect taxes from everyone and make Pakistan very rich so we never have to beg again, and he will immediately stop taking aids from America and start taking it from China instead. And also, most importantly, he won't have anything to do with any corrupt, lota type politician from PML-N or PML-Q or PPP or ANP or MQM or anyone. No wonder they are all quacking in their boots with fear, these corrupt lota politicians. You should've seen them—so many of them were at the rally and you know, one or two of them were even sitting on the stage besides him. As if they were honoured guests or something! Who gave them permission to sit there, haan? Just look at them, besharams! Someone should tell Imran. I bet you he never even noticed that they are creeping into his party. Itna voh sachee honest sa hai na . . .

December 2011

'Memogate' scandal bodes ill for Zardari
Butterfly yearns for the staff at Downton Abbey

If I could have one thing to make my life easier, bus sirraf one thing, you know what it would be? No, it wouldn't be a hotel size generator. It wouldn't be immigration visa to Canada even. That would be very nice, I admit, but not as nice as what I really want. The thing that I really, really want is the head bearer in that TV series *Downtown Abbey*. Kya naam tha uss ka? Haan, Car Son. Now if I could have Car Son, my life would become so easy, so easy keh poocho hi na. Him and that housekeeper, Mrs Use. Then tau I would be least bothered about anything.

Hai, how nicely they manage everything! Nothing ever gets stolen. Nothing ever breaks. No vases, no glasses, no plates, nothing even cracks. The silver is always shining, the flowers are hamesha fresh and the knives are never laid on the left and the kantaas on the right like my stuppid Raheem does even now after three years of me standing on his head. No maid ever answers the phone and says, 'Begum Sahiba pot pur bethi hain.' Lady Cora never has to be in the middle

146

of any larhais between the chowkidaar and the sweeper, no maid ever bursts into the sitting room and starts howling that she has been possessed by jinns, nor does her lady's ship ever have to hear: 'Bibi ji, meri maan mar gayee hai, please aik haftay ki chhutti chahye.' Everything Mr Car Son and Mrs Use manage behind the screens.

All the naukars are dressed so nicely in their uniforms. In fact, the male naukars are so smart, so smart, they tau almost look as if *they* are maaliks. In fact, now that I'm having I might as well have *all* the naukars from Downtown Abbey. As Mummy always says if you are doing, do fully only. Otherwise don't do.

That Anna who looks after Lady Mary, she makes her hair so nicely, no? Her tau I'll take just now only. But I have to say that Cora's old naukrani—voh Oh Brian nahin thi?—she was a bit of a sarrhi boti. And she gave Cora a miscarriage, remember? And it was a baby boy also, after all those girls. The male hair that Robert Saab wanted so badly. No baba, Oh Brian can stay in Downtown only.

And what about that bearer who is a gay? That good looking chalaak one, who is always plodding and planning against Anna and her husband, Bakes. What was his name now? Yes, Wheel Barrow, him also I don't think so I'll keep. Too much of a fasaadi. And bhai, I tau have to think of my young son also. So no question, Wheel Barrow's not coming anywhere near my kothi.

Bakes is a bit bore, going about with his stick like that—all the time, thak thak thak, I think so he'd get on my nerves. And I don't think so Janoo needs him. Janoo is very independent minded, na. He can button up his own shirt himself and khair cuff lings tau he doesn't wear even. But Mrs Pat More, the khansamah, I'm a bit double minded about her. Chalo, I'll take her, because she's very duty conscious, but I'll have to send her to Mummy's cook to learn how to make aloo gosht and kebabs and haleems and all. I wonder if she has taste in her hands?

Hai, but I'm forgetting the driver, Brazen. Remember, the one who deduces Lady Sea Bill, the youngest daughter of the house? Him tau I'll never take in a million years even. Uff, just look at his guts! Romancing that sweet si, innocent si bacchi like that! Such a namak haram, no?

Vaisay socha jaye tau really the only ones worth having are Car Son and Mrs Use. If I'd lived anywhere near Downtown Abbey, I'd have stolen them long since. But the other naukars, Brazen and Oh Brian and Wheel Barrow and Bakes and all, my shoe even won't invite them to Gulberg. Anna I still like but I don't think so she'd come without Bakes. And quite honestly, at this point in my life I have no time for nakhraas, okay? If she doesn't want to come on her own to my kothi in Gulberg, tau na aaye. I damn care. Besides my Filipina, she also knows waxing and threading and I think so Lady Mary hasn't made Anna learn any of that. And not blow drying either. So, bus, Car Son and Mrs Use only, that's all.

January 2012

Imran Khan holds massive rally in Karachi
Janoo jealous of Imran, suspects Butterfly

Bhai, I'm tau joining Imran's party. Why? Because I was at this really glam shaadi in Karachi two days before his Karachi waali rally and everyone was talking of how they're going to join him only.

'Bus, bohat ho gya hai,' they were saying. 'We've tried Nawaz and we've tried Benazir and what did they give us? A big fat zero, that's what. So now we're going to try Imran.'

Reminded me a little bit of when my two usual waxing women, Sheela and Nichho, both raised their rates just like that ('Bibi, barhi mehngai ho gayee hai, 500 ki ub zehar bhi nahin milti') and so I decided to try this other girl, Meena, who kept asking for a chance ('Aap aik dafa try tau maarein') and she came and ripped the skin off my armpit. Had to wear full sleeved for two full months and that also in July and August. And don't even ask what I had to do for deodorant . . .

Not that Imran is going to rip off my armpits. He tau is so honest, so uptight (or was it upwrite?) and so very nice. And if you want proof, look how nicely he dies his hair. Honestly, sixty years old and not a hint of white from anywhere. Maybe his smooth sayer, the same one who told him he will be leader of free world, maybe he also told him where to find his hairdresser. Maybe I should also go to same smooth sayer. Wonder what nice, nice things he'll tell me? That I'm going to be the Maggie Catcher of Asia. Or maybe the Princess Diana of Pakistan.

Haan, so going back to the wedding, all these really fashiony sophisty type ladies, na, all wearing two, two, three, three lakh ka joras and diamonds as big as ice cubes, they were all saying that they're joining him because they want change, na. I think so, but this is just between you, me and the four walls, they also have secret crushes on him. Honestly, you just see the way they flatter their eyelashes at him and spout their lips and go all giggly when he's around. Vaisay I can't really blame them. I mean, given a choice between Altaf Bhai and Nawaz Sharif, he wins hands down, in the looks ki department, I mean. And these ladies' husbands, all big cigar smoking business typhoons with bullet proofed Mercs, they also threw big party for Imran and pledged their undrying support—as long as he gives them the changes they want.

Because Janoo is into politics big time and he thinks I never do any politics ki talk, I went straight away and told him how my khaata peeta friends were all wanting change.

'What change do they want?' he asked in that sarrhial voice. 'They want to start paying their taxes for a change? They want to declare their assets for a change? Start repaying their bad loans for a change?'

Talking to Janoo is also such time waist. He calls Imran the army's It Boy. Between you, me and the four walls, I think so Janoo is jealous. Like Imran, he's also an Oxen, na. But unlike Imran, Janoo never became a cricketing legion, nor a hospital saint, nor a Nelson Medallion of Pakistan and also, nor did he marry an English airess. You know, Imran's right when he says that the only reason these westoxified sarrhial septics like Janoo don't support his party is because they didn't get to date all the English khaata peeta girls that he dated. And they're dying of saarh. Bus, that's all.

Febuary 2012

US drone kills twenty-one
Butterfly embarrassed by Kulchoo's interest in calligraphy

Between you, me and the four walls, I'm a little bit worried about Kulchoo. You know he's always been arty type, na, more into history than chemistry, but now he's become a bit too much arty. He's also gone crazy about playing the sexophone. Spends hours and hours practising, when frankly speaking, he should be doing his studies, specially econ. Second, he's started doing cally graphy. Why he can't play polo ya phir tennis? At least those things American university wallahs have heard about. Who knows or cares about cally graphy, yaar? And also nowdays with printers shinters in everyone's house, who even needs it, batao? Why does our Kulchoo have to sit across legged on the floor with a qalam and a takhti, learning how to write from an Urdu medium ustaad who comes on a motor bike? Not even a car. As Mummy was saying if it's a hobby he wants, why can't he buy a thoroughly bred horse and go riding, haan?

I was getting really worried kay he was becoming loser type and what kind of carrier choices he's going into when

I was so reliefed, so reliefed kay don't even ask. He put up a big poster in his room with the slogan 'Occupy Wall Street' and I thought, Allah ka shukr, mera beta is going to be a Wall Street ka banker working for banks like Golden Sacks and Merril Flinch and he's getting ready to occupy it. When I proudly told Janoo he laughed his head off and said, 'My son's a young man with a conscience. He wants to destroy Wall Street, not join it!' Uff, it's all Janoo's fault. I tau blame him entirely. Cent per cent. It's he only who's been putting too much of importance on music and drama and art shart and useless things like that, as if Kulchoo's going to become, God forbid, an artist or actor or some other kind of loser when he grows up.

Don't get me wrong, okay? I'm not like those pushy desi mothers who only want their sons to be doctors or lawyers. I'm not at all against arts. In fact, I'm arty type myself. I did art for my O levels, na, and I think so it really helped me because everyone says my dinner table arrangements, they are so artistic, but really, I mean, Kulchoo's not going to be laying tables, is he? Nor is he going to be playing the sexophone in restaurants like a do paisay ka bechara while other people tuck into an expensive dinner. And nor is he a girl who's doing these things for time pass till she gets married. No ji, my son is going to be a politician or banker and of course, a big land lord like his father.

March 2012

Baloch leaders in no mood to accept talks offer
Butterfly goes on a diet

Do you know Dr Jamal Kamal? Janoo says he's a quack but I say he is a foreign ka returned diet doctor, ji. How do I know? Because I saw photos in his office of him standing outside a building in abroad and a sign outside the building saying Imperial College, which even illitreds know is a top door science college in London, so if *that* doesn't prove he's a top ka doctor then I don't know what does. Besides, he's made Baby half her size. He put her on a diet of lemon and hot water four times a day for six days and he charged her twenty-five thou for that. But it was money well spent because Baby, she lost so much weight, so much weight that she had to go to hospital but when I went to see her there she beckoned me close and when I leaned down she whispered to me in this rasping, horse voice and, I'm sorry to say, stinking breaths, that she's ordered a new jora from Kami. In XXS.

So immediately I also made a beehive for Dr JK and what he did, he looked me up and down and tapped his four head three times with his finger and did calculations on his computer and finally he joined up the tips of his fingers and after a long paws in which he stared first at the ceiling, then at the floor and finally at me, he said I had a unique case of middle aged spread. 'Haw hai, doctor saab,' I said, 'I thought middle aged spread was something you draped on your sofa or bicchhaoed on your double bed.' Turns out it's what happens to your hips and stomach when you cross forty.

But apparently mine's an extra special unique case for which he gave me a special personalized diet plan. So my personalized plan said lemon and hot water four times a day for a week. I asked him how it was different to Baby's and he said Baby's was for six days. And it costed me twenty thou but I went home happy because, one, even a foreign returned doctor recognizes I'm unique and, two, because I'm going to bid fear well to my middle aged spread and, three, I undercut Baby by five thou.

So the minute Janoo left for Sharkpur, I started my diet. If he'd been around he would have force-fed me. That way he's very bossy, na. So anyways, it's been four days since I've been doing it and I'm laid up in bed because every time I try and stand I feel like I'm going to pass away and my hair has started falling out by the truck load and it hurts when I breathe and my mouth tastes like the floor of a lemonade factory on which a lot of labourers have been walking in dirty Ugh boots and my tongue looks like it's wearing a fur coat and I'm seeing double, double and basically I think I'm going to die but at least at my funeral I'll be wearing size eight ki J Brand skinny jeans. And Mulloo will be so jay. Oho baba, jealous, and I'll be so happy . . .

March 2012

Pakistan wins Oscar award for acid victims documentary
Butterfly suggests a change of name for Gaddafi Stadium

Chalo, it's official now. Us and the Indians, we are at last equal, equal. If they won Oscar for their slump kids then we won Oscar for our acid victims. And I think so the Iranians also won an Oscar for a film all about a married couple who are always fighting and wanting a divorce and pushing people down the stairs and telling lies and all. I think so it was called *The Separation* or *The Divorce* or something like that. I was so happy that mashallah say look how well we've done and how much the world is clapping for us.

And also I was glad that Sharmeen Obaid Chinoy had worn such a nice designer jora to the Oscars to show the world how fashiony and sophisty we are. And that, thanks God, she wasn't one of these NGO types with undied hair and khaddar kurtas and dirty silver jewellery and brown leather chappals with feet that have never seen a paddy cure.

But Mulloo, she says I'm stuppid for feeling happy.

'Don't you know that Amreekans never give us desi types any prizes for nice, nice, happy, happy things?' she said.

'Only for sad things which show us up in bad lights. It's all a big conspiracy against us. They want us to look poor and illitred and backwards. So they can feel rich and educated and forwards. It's all about them being up, up and us all down, down. All the Indian and Pakistani books that the goras are giving Bookish Prize to and Common Health prize to, they are also always about our poors and how we rich types never look after them and basically just kuchlo them under our feet.'

Naturally I'd never read any of those bore books so I'd never thought of all that, so I just frowned in an intelligent sa way and said, 'Hmmm.' But then I remembered and I said, 'But didn't they give Noble Prize to that Pakistani doctor?'

'Which doctor?' she asked. 'The plastic surgeon?'

'No baba, the one who made some discovery in civics.'

'Who are you meaning? I don't remember any doctor shoctor who got Noble Prize.'

So later I was telling Janoo and he said, 'You mean Dr Abdus Salaam, the physicist.'

Haan, tau what did I say? That he was dentist?

'In any other country he would have been honoured with titles and medals,' Janoo said. 'He would have had colleges named after him. And streets and schools and chairs at universities. And here, just because he was an Ahmedi, his name's been erased.'

So then, just like that, I had an idea. I said, 'Can't we name Gaddafi Stadium in Lahore after him? Seeing kay Gaddafi has now gone to Allah Mian.'

Janoo gave me sarrhial look and said, 'Dr Salaam was a scientist. Not an athlete.'

Haw, so Gaddafi was an athlete? Look at me, I didn't even know. And here I was thinking he was a general. Maybe he was both things, like a lot of famous people are. For instant I've heard Cameroon is a cyclist in his spare time and the Queen—oho baba, Elizabeth only—she's a jockey and Jackie Kennedy, apparently she was an interiors waali, she did up White House, na. So maybe Dr Abdus Salaam, maybe when he wasn't doing science he was a long jumper or even a marathong runner. Bhai, I've tau learnt one thing from life and that's this: kissi ka kuch pata nahin hota.

April 2012

Sectarian militancy thriving in Balochistan
Butterfly hears of friend's divorce

Mummy's right. It's a curse to be sensitive. Take me only. So much worrying and anxiety I do keh I can't sleep at night. I can't switch on TV when I'm lying awake at night because Janoo is such a light sleeper. So I decided I'll go and buy some magazines to read in the night. So I went to a bookshop in Liberty to pick up the latest issue of *Vogue* and *Good Times* vaghera. In the bookshop I ran into Bubbly. Poor thing, she's decided to divorce her hubby, Usman. Haan, but what else could she do after he disgraced her like that in front of all her friends and family?

See, it was Usman's fiftieth birthday and when he came downstairs to have breakfast, he expected Bubbly and the kids to wish him. And make out a big deal of him. But they completely ignore karoed him. Then he thought his parents and sisters would call during the day to wish him. They even did nothing. So, all day long Usman was in a skulk in his office. But in the evening, just before he was going home, his secretary—who apparently is a pretty young thing in heels and a high pony tail—said, 'Happy birthday, sir' and gave him a chhota sa present, like a pen or something. Then she said, 'Let's go and have a cup of tea at the café next door.' Happily, he trotted off with her.

After tea she said, 'You're such a sweet boss. I'd really like to do something for you. Why don't you come over to my place for a cozy dinner, haan?' Bus, Usman tau was so happy, so happy that don't even ask. He sucked in his stomach, loosened his tie and off he went with her. At her place—she has a cute sa flat in Defence, which I think so her parents bought her—there were flowers in the living room and scented candles and dim, dim si lights and she asked Usman to relax and make himself comfortable while she went to the bedroom.

Next thing he knew, the secretary, Bubbly, the kids, his parents, sisters, brothers-in-law, Mulloo, Bobby, Pinky and Taj all burst into the room with a cake and candles, shouting, 'Surprise!' Trouble is, poor Usman was sitting on the sofa in his birthday suit . . .

May 2012

Imran asks PML-N to resign from assemblies
Butterfly unimpressed by Sunny's Brazilian gift

Sunny has just come back from a chhutti in Brazeel. She's brought suitcases full of semi precious stones from there—topazes and amethists and garnets and parrydots. Says she'll have big, big sets made by goldsmith. Yearrings and rings and lockets vaghera. Such a cheapster show-offer, she is. So I told her saaf saaf, I said, 'I tau only wear emeralds and rubies and diamonds, baba. No cheap semis for me, thank you very much.'

Guess what she brought for me and for Mulloo? Plastic ki havai chappals, if you please. She says Brazeel ki havai chappals are so trendy, so trendy that even Angelina Jolly and Bad Pitts wear them. I think so they're called Haivaans. They can be called Shaitaans for all I care. As far as I'm concerned, the only people who wear havai chappals are dhobis and sweepers. And thanks God I'm neither.

Anyways, Sunny was saying Brazeel also has lots of poors, who all live in kachi abadis called fever-elas. Before she went everyone said to her keh na, don't take even a chandi ki ring

161

with you because the second you step off the plane you get mugged. In the arrivals ki lounge only they mug you. And Sunny, because she feels naked without her diamond solitaires, she bought some fake ones from Icchhra and she put those inside her ears before she went. And then she wasn't even mugged shugged. She says it was all proper ganda against the Brazeelians. 'They're actually very shareef,' she said. I said inside my heart only, 'Haan, as if muggers are all cracks that they can't tell twenty rupees kay glass chips when they see them.'

But Sunny says their poors are very jolly, happy go lucky types. All day they are doing surfing and dancing (these black types, they love dancing, na, I think so it's in their jeans only) and playing bolly ball and foot ball on the Copper Cabana beach. Not like our poors who are constantly complaining and crying and killing each other and us also. She also says the Brazeelian poors have ultra gorge bodies and everyone wears nothing. Or nest to nothing and they all look so tabahi in their string bikinis and chhoti, chhoti si shorts.

'Haw, Sunny,' I said, 'no offence, but then you tau must have stuck up like a soar thump.'

'At least I travel, darling,' she said to me, smiling fakely. 'Not like you who only ever goes to boring old London. Which to me is just like my backyard. So many times I've been coming and going.'

Look at Sunny. So catty, so vicious. Just because her husband has made two paisas she's started putting on so many hairs and graces. I could have made thousand, thousand responds to her but you know what? I didn't. And why? Because I'm a khandani from a good bagground, who'd never in a month of Mondays give plastic ki chappals to my sweepress even, let alone my kitty party friends who are, natch, all khaata peeta khandanis. But as you all are fully knowing, poor Sunny, she has neither my bagground, nor my breathing, nor my class . . .

May 2012

Trade routes to open between India and Pakistan
Butterfly wants to visit an ashram

Bhai, I've tau always said that India is my Most Flavoured Nation. Now guvmunts on both sides have also copied me and opened up trade roots between us and them. So thanks God we can all become rich now. Talking of rich, many Indian businessmen came to Lahore for this seminal called Aman ki Asha. Janoo went to listen to their speeches but I went to see Prameshwar Godrej. She's just like us—Punjabi, tall, good looking, wheatish complexion. I pointed her out to Mulloo, who'd gone with me to the seminal.

'There she is! I know Prameshwar Godrej,' I said.

Mulloo snapped back, 'But does she know you?'

Uffff! Some people vaisay are too much eaten up by jealousy!

Suna hai that in return for our cement ki boris and lawn ka joras, India is going to give us lots of lovely bijli and other nice, nice things like Shahrukh Khan and Paan Bahar and kanji worm saris and cars kay parts and so much of steel, so much of steel keh we can put railings all round Pakistan if we want.

Apparently they are crazy for our foods across the boarder. I told Janoo that please put all your onions and mangoes and wheat sheet and whatever else you grow into a truck and send it to Amrit Sir today only. He said mangoes are not ready yet. I said, who cares, baba? Don't you remember that song Kulchoo used to sing when he was a doddler, 'Ready or not here I come . . .' Vaisay between you and me and the four walls, you know the problem with Janoo, na? All his get up and go has got up and gone. If it wasn't for me, sachee, he tau would be a total non identity.

Also visa constrictions to India are going to be relaxed. So instead of going bar bar to bore Delhi I can book myself into one of their super luxurious ashrams (but with twenty-four hour servants) in a romantic sa quiet type village with palm trees and lotus ponds and air-conditioned huts. You know the type of place where they give you daily enemas till you feel like the world has fallen out of your bottom? And they do your massages till your yatras are talking to your chakras and your agni is talking to your jugni and you are doing ahimsa morning, noon and night. And they make you eat little Your Vedic pills and portions made from herbal cow pats and crushed snail shells and powdered mosquito wings and other vegetarian delights. And they make you sit across legged on a rush ka mat and close your eyes and chant 'Om Shanti Om' till you feel like slapping someone, but gently only. And at the end of it all you come out totally retoxed and your inner light is shining like a hello gen bulb and you're looking like Ashwariya (before baby, but). Now you see why India is my most flavoured nation?

June 2012

UK celebrates sixtieth anniversary of Queen Elizabeth's coronation
Butterfly resolves to have a pop concert followed by fireworks at her next birthday

Must say, what a zabardast party the London ka goras laid out for their malika, no? So many different, different functions. Almost as good as what Janoo calls the 'late, great basant'. I tau watched everything from start to finish on Kulchoo's computer. Vaisay I think so the Queen could have smiled a bit more. She looked a bit sarrhial through out. And why wasn't she wearing a crown, haan? Least she could have done. But thanks God, Kate looked nice in that red outfit. But if I'd been her I would have carried a nice red Birkin to complete my look. But maybe she didn't because as Mulloo says, Birkin tau itna sakht common ho gya hai, every wanna bee begum has five, five, six, six.

But one thing I was very impress with. Did you see how the Queen and her husband, the Duck of Edinburgh, the way they stood all those hours on the royal boat all down the river? Imagine, yaar, she deep into her eighties and he almost hundred years old and standing so long without even holding on to anything, let alone leaning on anything? If The Old Bag, Janoo's mother, had seen it, she would have said they must have eaten lots of desi ghee as kids. It strengthens your bones, na. I said to Aunty Pussy that you tau must be remembering the Queen's carnation sixty years ago? And she said, 'Hai, jaan, how could I? I was only five then!' I swear, what a bear faced liar she is! She's even older than Sir Clip Richards.

Vaisay did you see how he was leaping around on the stage at the concert outside Buckingham Palace? Like he was twenty or something? And Grace Jones, like a pehelwan, I swear! Such big muscly thighs she has. Janoo says she's at least sixty-five. Thanks God she didn't take off her big plastic headdress because I think so if she had, her plastic face would have come off with it also. And did you see the fire works? And the lights ka show? Uff, total tabahi! I'll also have one just like that for my next birthday. And the pop concert also. And next day they had this big lunch jiss pay total ordinaries like gardeners from Regent Park and nurses from hospitals were invited to come and sit with khandanis like Kate and Queen vaghera. Imagine!

June 2012

Bahria Town developer Malik Riaz implicated in massive corruption scandal
Butterfly muses on Arab Spring

When people first began talking of Arab Springs, I thought they were talking of a spa—an Arab frenchise, you know, a bit like Maroush in London with branches on Edgewear Road and Knightsbridge. So I thought Arab Springs was a chain of spas with branches in Tunisya and Egypt and Libya and all. I shouldn't say, because they are our Muslim sisters, but Arab women are very hairy, na. All the time they are threading and waxing and sugaring and all. That's why I thought Arab Springs was a spa where they got their legs done and their eyebrows and their upper lips. And also their colonic irritation and their massages. So when people said that in Bahrain and in Yemen it hadn't taken off and that royal families there had opposed it very much, I thought maybe the women there are not needing so much of waxing. Anyways, under those heavy black niqabs, who's to see if your upper lips are threaded or not?

And then suddenly it donned on me—now don't ask bore questions like how and why—that all these remonstrations in Tahrir Square and all the bombings in Libya and all the killing shilling in Syria, *this* is Arab Springs. Why it should be called spring and not spring, summer, autumn and winter, seeing it's lasted years is anyone's guest. So I asked Janoo, I asked him why spring lasts a whole year in Arab places and why it's only ten days long in Pakistan? Then he told me slowly and quietly like I was some backwards child, that Arab Spring is not a season, it's actually a big fight between Arab peoples and their guvmunts. Respite ruling for thirty, thirty, forty, forty years their rulers were enjoying too much to vacate their kursis and so the people who hadn't been enjoying at all for the last forty years were fighting with them and saying no, no, you must go now. And they call it spring because it's meant to be an awakening.

You tau know how much broad minded I am, but between you, me and the four walls, I think so all these peoples from sandy type places, they're a little bit backwards. I know Dubai has biggest malls and also the tallest sky scrapper and that Saudi Arabia is all air-conditioned and completely covered with marble but imagine waking up after forty years, like you were Sleeping Beauty or someone. What I mean is keh instead of sitting around suffering silently for forty years, why they didn't arrange a little plane crash like we did for General Zia after eleven years, haan? That way everyone has a nice change. We don't get bored of seeing same grinning face on our TV screens for forty years and also the army wallahs, the generals and the captains and all, they also come out of their barracks and get a chance to make even more money and march about in their uniforms. So why the Arabs don't do like us?

And also when we were seeing Egyptians on TV guarding their neighbourwoods from looters and thievers, I must say I was tau very disappointed. The only arms they had were kitchen knives and baseball bats. Now if it had been Pakistan, every household would have had at least two, two Kalashnicoughs, if not a rocket launcher or even a missile or two. No wonders, their spring has dragged on for a whole year. And Libya is meant to be so rich and all, and it didn't even have an atom bomb. Honestly! Now you know why I think they are backwards?

Janoo is very excited that there are stirrings of Arab Spring in Saudi also. Janoo is not a fan of their royal family, na. I'm not minding the Saudis so much because, thanks God, I don't have to live there and receive hundred lashes for driving and go about dressed all in black like a ninja. The only thing I mind about them is that they are a little bit rude when you go to do Hajj. And their religious police, I'm sorry to say, has no manners at all. I think so they are not very much educated. Because you know they can't even tell the difference between those of us who are affording types and are doing Hajj in the laps of luxury and the poors who've shrimped and saved all their lives to do a cut price one. They shove and push everyone the same. I know they're not educated but at least they could show a little bit of respect to people from khandani baggrounds. And also they are putting up madrassahs in every village in our country and turning all our innocent bhooka nanga unemployeds into vicious Wahhabi Al-Qaedas. I hope so Arab Spring comes tomorrow into Saudi.

July 2012

Kidnappers kill miners, doctor; dump bodies
Butterfly nurses Mummy through illness

Mummy's been ill, na. Haw, didn't you know? She tau, poor thing, has been so ill, so ill keh poocho hi na. For full three weeks, she's been ill. Ub tau mashallah say she's *much* better but in between I swear she was touchy and go. It all started when she complained of chest pains and tight, tight si breathing. Thinking it must be heart, I took her straight away to Lahore's top ka cardiacologist, Dr Sheheryar. He did her BCG and told us she didn't have heart.

'I could have told you that without charging a single penny,' murmured Janoo but apart from karaoing him a cold si look, I ignored. Kya faeda, of rising to the bake?

So I took Mummy home but still her chest was paining. I told her not to eat khaanas like corn on the cop and fried mutters which give her gas and also to not think sarrhial thoughts. Next morning her maid called me up and said please to come immediately because Begum Saab Ji has raving fever and she's hello cinating. So at once I rushed over to discover that her breaths were coming all fast, fast and choked, choked.

172

I took her to Omar hospital and there the doctor put on those tubes that doctors put inside their ears and listened to her chest and also checked her signs and systems and said she had newmonia.

'Haw, in this heat?' I said. 'With this much of load shedding? She should be having heat stroke, not newmonia.' But then I remembered that Mummy's always liked being different, na.

She was in hospital for full two weeks getting anti-bioticks and asteroids through tubes and trips vaghera and then we brought her home. But the doctors said she must make sure that she has lots of rest (as if we were going to make her mow the lawn and wash the carpets!). They also gave us a list of medicines as long as Aunty Pussy's tongue to give to her morning, noon and night. Obviously we are giving but I swear it's not easy with the guests. Since she's come back we've had a constant scream of guests all coming to ask after her and say that thanks God Allah nay unko rakh liya. I want to tell them that *I'm* the one you should be asking after. After all, *I'm* the one who's done all bhaag dorh and all that raat ki hospital duty (well, between you, me and the four walls, I used to send my maid most of the nights because it's such a treat for her, na, to spend the whole night on an armchair in an air-conditioned room) but you know me, so self defecating and publicity shy, majaal hai that I should take any credits.

But Mummy's friends, honestly, they're charhoing so much on my nerves now. Aunty Sona, who's been at school with her since the dawn of time, she announced the other day that we should immediately stop all these medicines that we're giving because they are very heat creating and they will boil her insides and that we should just give her karelay ka juice and nothing else because that is cooling. When I told her that the doctor has subscribed the medicines she said don't listen to the doctors. They're jahils. Listen to me. Then Aunty Billa, who's become a bit of a fundo recently and has forbidden Coke from her house because she says it contains sharaab, she came and said we should soak a paper full of special prayers in a glass of water and make her drink that and we'd see with our own eyes how she'd leap straight out of the bed and on to a prayer mat. But Aunty Juicy, she's Mummy's old bridge partner, she tau really took the cakes. She kept talking of Mummy as if she'd died or gone into a comma or something. 'Kitni nicely tum nay usski look after ki thi. Allah kitna savaab day ga. Chalo, jo hona tha ho gya. Allah ki marzi.' Honestly. Mummy better get better quickly nahin tau I'm going to end up in hospital by the time her friends are through with me.

August 2012

London hosts Olympic Games
Butterfly decides against going to London

I was thinking of maaroing a quick chakkar of London in July but then I heard that all the flats and hotels were being hogged by Arabs who'd all descented on London aik dum because August mein tau the Holy Month of Al Ramadan was coming and for that they had to be home to keep rozas and earn savaabs and make numbers with Allah Mian. So through out July the all-night casinos on Edgewear Road were full to the grim with Arabs. The Edgewear Road ones are their favourites because you get served halaal gosht over there, na. So you can gamble with a clean conscious.

Anyways, by the time the Arabs left, the Olympick had come and then tau rest of whole world was descenting on London. So I thought, chalo baba, might as well stay behind and say my prayers and keep my rozas and be holy.

And thanks God I stayed because turns out hardly anyone went to London. Suna hai all the shops are lying empty and streets are wearing deserted looks and owls are hooting in the hotels and all the goras can talk about is Hussain Bold and

More Farah and rowing showing and other bore, bore games. Janoo and Kulchoo were tarhpoing to go but turns out their visas have run out and about and Janoo can't face all the bhaag dorh you have to do to get another one. So they've bought a thousand-inch waala TV on which they watch bedminton and bolly balls vaghera kay matches night and day. Losers jaisay.

Meanwhiles I'm doing Al Ramadan in my usual underslated style. My Al Ramadan wardrope is so simple—all Swiss voile in pail, pail say colours. Edged with white lace. I tau really don't understand why people moan so much about Al Ramadan being in summers. There's nothing to it, yaar. You just keep your fast, say your prayers, give the servants order for iftaar, draw your curtains, put your AC on full blast (just make sure the servants keep the generator filled with oils) and sleep all day. You get your servants to wake you up an hour before iftaar. You bathe, get blow dried, change into a pail white Swiss voile jora and stroll into your dining room where table is covered with biryani and kebabs and haleems and so on and so fourth and you greet your iftaar guests. After that you go to a taravee GT. Do hello hi with all the gang, say a few taravees and if it's the weekend you stay till sehri, have a small sehri GT and then go home and sleep. Bus. Easy peasy.

September 2012

**French magazine publishes topless photos of Kate Middleton
Butterfly thinks Prince William is a wimp**

I think so Prince William (oho, Queen ka grandson, baba, Charles ka beta), he's turned out to be completely beghairat. Look at him. This trashy French magazine takes photos of his wife Kate Middleclass in topless and actually prints them and he can't do a thing about it. Beghairat! If you ask me, he shouldn't look left, he shouldn't look right. He should take a leap out of our mullahs' handbook and go straight away and burn down the French embassy in London to punish that French photographer and that dirty French magazine. And if he can't burn down the embassy then at least he should burn some French restaurants and if he can't even burn the French restaurants then he should go to Harrods and burn down the Channel ka counter and beat up the make up girls who serve behind it (never mind if they're English, or Polish, or even, God forbid, Pakistani—it will serve them right for doing naukri of Frenchies).

And I think so Prince William should also burn tyres and disrupt traffic in front of Selfridges and Harvey Nicholas for stocking Dior, YSL, Channel and other French brands. He should also stop anyone driving a Renault or a Citrong and drag them out of their cars and beat them up before setting fire to their cars. He should beat up all the schoolchildren who study French in England and set fire to their textbooks. He should teach everyone who has anything to do with France such a lesson, such a lesson that not even their grandchildren will forget.

Mein tau kehti hoon, Prince William should even come to French Beach in Karachi and burn the sea over there also. He should show the French who's who and what's what, no? Everyone will do so much of wah wah of him and have so much respect for him after that. Vaisay I think so it was totally beghairat of him to sue the magazine in French courts when he could be stroking anger outside. I mean, is he a man or a mouse? And also I'd like to ask why the British army's top ka general hasn't come out and complained to French ka army chief kay bhai, why you have abused our Sovereignty, haan? I heard with my own ears Janoo saying that one day Prince William will be Sovereign of England and so Kate Middleclass will be Sovereignty. Printing her nangi photos is obviously violation of British Sovereignty and William kay liye doob marnay ka maqaam hai if you have a ghairat mand perspective on life like us type of people.

I tau just don't understand why William has to be such a bakri, honestly. And just look at the French! This is the thanks they give to the English for buchaowing them from Hitler, haan? And if you say anything to them aagay say they shrug and say, 'Say la we!' Their cheeks!

October 2012

Malala Yousafzai shot in the head by Taliban
Mulloo insistent that Taliban not guilty

I can't tell you what happened in my heart when I heard about Malala. So sad I was, na, little si girl, so fair and pretty with light, light eyes and that shy sa smile. Just going in her school ki van. And a beardo stops her and shoots her in the head. Just like that.

Just the day before I was talking to Mulloo about Talibans ka rule and Imran Khan's peace march to Waziristan to stop the drawns.

'Imran's a Pathan and knows fully what he's talking about when he says that we should all make peace with Talibans,' I said. Mulloo agreed, but as usual, even when she agrees with me she has to make her own points. She thinks so she has special knowledge on everything. So she said, 'It's not just Imran, bhai. Even all these goras are wanting to make peace with Talibans. Americans are wanting. Canadians are wanting. Brits are wanting.'

I was all for Imran's march against drawns with glam goras to Waziristan, and his sayings that we should make peace with

Talibans. I thought shukkar hai, at least someone's giving off positive wibes about Pakistan. But then I saw the news about Malala on TV and my heart stank.

Janoo said in his depressing voice, 'I suppose you want to make peace with the man who shot that little girl.'

'Taubah!' I cried. 'Trust you to always say stuppid things.'

But that night when I was talking to Mulloo on the phone, I said in a whisper so that Janoo couldn't hear, 'But Mulloo, how can we make peace with Taliban who shot Malala? What if they do it again and again? They've tau repeated hundred times that they're against girls' education and will kill all girls who go to school and burn down all the schools also.'

Mulloo said, 'You know who's shot Malala? It's the Amreekans. They want to give Pakistan a bad name. Everybody knows their agencies are operating in our backside. We have to take a stand, but. We have to go out and show our faces for Malala and image of Pakistan.' Ever since Mulloo joined Imran, she's become very conscious of image of Pakistan.

In the morning I said my duas for Malala, and in the afternoon I put on my Puma kay joggers, packed my maids into the car and was ready to go out and show my face for Malala and the image of Pakistan. But then Mulloo called and said, 'Don't come to the protest at Press Club. That's been hijacked by liberal fascists.' Then again she called and said, 'And don't go to Charing Cross, it's a very rough sa crowd, all poors and Labour Party wallahs.' And then she called a third time and said, 'And when you get here, remember not to take the name of Talibans, we are just going to criticize drones.'

I suppose one has to do these things for one's country ka image. Being patriotic and all.

November 2012

Police hot on the tracks of auto thieves
Butterfly's neighbour harassed

Haw, you know what happened at our neighbours' yesterday? Not our real neighbours but our neighbours three doors down where the big garbage dump is? Yes, there only. It's a small house and in it lives this old lady, Apa Rahat—I think so once upon a time, she was lady doctor. Her husband is Late and her kids are abroad. I used to see her being driven in her small car by this ancient driver who finally copt it and then she got this new driver, young sa with brownish hair—I think so it was died. His name was Samuel. And you know, na, what that means. That he wasn't One of Us. Us Muslims, I mean.

Next door to this lady is this house with a marble pyramid. It's got a huge PML flag flying on top (two months ago the flag was PTI and three months before that it was PPP) and ten-foot high iron kay gates and guards with guns and moustaches that curl up at the ends. I think so owners are feudals. My cook says they've got lands near Sargodha.

Anyways, three days ago, Apa Rahat was being reversed

out of her house in her car and outside her house the feudal servants were laying some wires on the road and they waved at the car to stop and Samuel didn't see and drove over the wires. Bus. The next day the guards arrived at Apa Rahat's house and asked her to hand over Samuel. They said they had a store to settle with him. Luckily, Apa Rahat had sent him to the market and she told them he'd gone home and Promise By God she didn't know where he lived. So muttering darkly they left.

Next day, Apa Rahat's feudal neighbour plus guards came striving up her driveaway. Apa Rahat's heart tau stank. Samuel was in her store room fixing a bulb. She locked him in and went downstairs to offer her guests chai pani. They said they didn't want chai shai, they wanted the Christian. Except they didn't call him Christian they called him that other Ch word. So Apa Rahat, she stammered out that after what happened, she was so angry with Samuel she'd sacked him herself only and now he was gone. The feudal kept staring at her silently and finally he snorted like an angry bull and left. So Apa Rahat crept upstairs and unlocked Samuel. She waited for the dark and snuggled him out in a burka, with two months celery and said please don't come back. Samuel wept and said he'd got his job after six months of searching and he had five children, and she said send your wife to me and I'll get her tubes tied.

When Janoo heard he put his head in hands and said it was a sign of the times. I hope so he didn't mean I should also get my tubes tied.

November 2012

Declaration on protection of journalists signed
Butterfly visits her chiropodist

I've just come back from my foot doctor. He takes care of all my corns and onions, na. His shop is on the backside of Main Market and it's called Feetish Footcare. I've heard some foot doctors, they handle your feet very suggestingly, na, stroking and massaging and all. But thanks God, my foot man is very shareef. He's never familiar with my feet. Vaisay tau I'm also very khandani with him. I call him docsaab even though he's as much a doctor as I am rocket scientist. But still, lehaaz bhi koi cheese hoti hai, baba . . .

While I was there Mulloo bounced in. Aik tau she's such a cheater cock. Always copying me. She used to go to Fancy Footworks but the minute she heard I have Feetish, she immediately did my cheating and switched to Feetish also. So anyways, she was banging on about Dubai where she'd gone to visit some paindu pastry cousin of hers who's moved there from Karachi to escape the fasaads and the khoon kharaba and all. She told me she tau was very disappointed with Dubai.

'Dubai Dubai nahin raha. It's become so full of foreigners. Jahan dekho foreigners. It's completely lost its charms.'

I wanted to say, 'A bit like Karachi then,' which I hear has become completely run over with Afghan Talibans and Arab Al-Qaedas. But I didn't say anything because ever since Mulloo's joined PTI, she won't hear a thing against the Talibans. And even if you say one tiny word against them she starts screaming that how would I like to be drawned by American drawns day and night, haan?

Anyways, when Mulloo finished conversing with herself, docsaab said in his usual shareef type low voice that he will be shutting his shop soon.

'But it isn't five o'clock yet,' I protested.

'No, not for today, forever,' said docsaab. 'I'm being forced to close down my business.'

'Haw hai,' Mulloo and I both said together. 'But why?'

'Because my son-in-law has grown a beard and he says if I carry on doing this fahaash, vulgar work, my nikah will break and because of that, he will be forced to divorce my daughter.' So I swung around to Mulloo and said, 'Now if you say the drawns are responsible for his son-in-law's beard I'm going to give you such a tight slap, such a tight slap that you'll have to grow a beard like your Taliban brothers to hide the bruise, okay?'

December 2012

Kate Middleton pregnant with royal baby
Butterfly saddened by nurse's suicide in London

I'm so happy, so happy that don't even ask. What for? Haw hai. For Kate Middleclass ki pregnancy, what else? I mean, it's not every day that a new hair to the throne is born, no? Maybe if it's a girl, she might even look like Diana, my most fave princess ever, even more than Princess Rania of Jordan. When she passed away I cried so much, so much that everyone said I became almost historical with grief. Itna mein nay feel kiya tha. For months after that I said special prayers for her every Thursday and fed the poors in her memory. So natch, I took it personally when Mummy said kay Princess Grace had a more namkeen face than Diana.

So I told her, I said, 'Oho Mummy, aik tau you are always talking of olden times. It's so bore to always have to listen to your endless stories of "hamaray zamanay mein". Anyways, who was this Princess Grace? Must have been a wife of Henry VIII or something.' But you know Mummy, na. Unfortunately, she can't take even itna sa criticism, no matter however well intented. So she immediately went into a skulk and started muttering about how no one has any respect for their olders any more and that in her hay days you never spoke back and you agreed with everything your olders said and that there's no lehaaz left in the world and no izzat is given to anyone and that's why the world is in such a mess.

Anyways, coming back to Kate, poor thing she's got very bad morning sickness. I hear, it's so bad, so bad that she's landed up in hospital. Just like me. When I was carrying Kulchoo I tau couldn't even look at Janoo's sisters, The Gruesome Twosome, without wanting to throw up. Us sensitive types, we are born to suffer, na.

And talking of suffering, hai, look at that poor Indian nurse who committed suicide after that hoax call to Kate's hospital from those two Australian TV kay stuppids. All she did was to put the call through but I think so she felt that she'd let the royal family down and she was so ashamed that she couldn't face anyone. I felt so bad for her and her family kay poocho hi na. Bechari, she must have been sole full sensitive type like me only.

January 2013

Temperatures dip to freezing point during coldest winter in decades
Butterfly yearns for global warming

I think so Kulchoo, my poor loser son, is the only young person left in Lahore. The only khaata peeta one, that is. All the other khaata peeta youngs, they have gone to Goya, India, where all the Goyans live. They've gone for that wedding, na. Of Kiran Chaudhry—oho baba, voh singer nahin hai?—to Riyaz Amlani, that Indian restaurant wallah.

Anyways, it was a really happening wedding. It opened with a tabahi bash at Uncle Jo's inner city haveli at which that DJ Hira Tareen put on the songs and Ali Zafar sang, and then a mehndi where that ancient fakir, Saeen Zahoor, twanged his cute sa ethnic sa instrument and sang all those cute, cute, purana, purana ethnic type songs in olden days ki Punjabi about unrequested love that no one understood but adored very much and also danced to in their tight mini dresses and their tattoos, and then there was a Devdas party at Royal Palm for which everyone dressed up as Bengali feudals from olden days, and then a qawwali at which Santoo qawwal sang, and then brunch, and then rukhsati, and then same all over again in India. I hope so there will be no rukhsati from there, but.

And the ones who didn't go to Goya went to Dubai and London for New Year's. Obviously, yaar, because yahaan tau koi scene nahin tha, na, celebration ka. I mean there was a nice party at Isbah's where me and Janoo went (Janoo sat in one corner playing with his Blueberry and me, I just sat in the other corner and gossiped about all the other guests with Mulloo). But aur tau there was nothing much to bright home about. Bus now there are two, three big weddings, one of the Mamdots and one of Noni and Salmi's son Kamil's and also a couple more. Uss ke ilava, the only thing that's happening is load shedding. Uff, so much of cold—going down to minus three at night, I swear. And then uss kay oopar no gas to heat your house or to have hot showers with and no bijli also. I've had to consort to having water heated on a wood burning choola in the outside ka kitchen and having that brought to my bathroom to have a balti bath with. The Americans are probing Uranus and I'm taking balti baths! I swear, vaisay look at Allah Mian, least he could have done was to give us warmish temperatures in our hour of need. I mean, where is global warning when we need it? Haan?

February 2013

**Despite warnings from extremists, Valentine's Day celebrated
with gusto in Lahore**
Butterfly wants an indoor pool

Yesterday I made a zara si, tiny si request to Janoo. I said to
him, dekho Janoo, Valentine Day's coming and I think so
you should give me a chhota sa present. I know it's not my
birthday so I won't ask for something big, but a chhota sa
present will be so nice.

He asked me what I wanted and I said keh please make
me a home cinema. So many nice, nice films are on these
days which we have to watch like bhooka nangas on our
forty-eight inch screen when everyone else—Sunny, Maha,
Baby vaghera—they all watch their parroted DVDs of
Less Miserables and *Lincoln* and *Zero Bark Thirty* and *Ah
Go* and *Race 2* and I don't know what, what else on at
least hundred inch ki screens. It doesn't look nice, na. And
even when Kulchoo's friends come they all first look at
our teeny tiny TV screen and then they look with pity
at Kulchoo. They don't say it but I know what they are

thinking: 'Hai bechara, he must be having such kanjoos makhi choos parents.'

'If you want to watch your films on really big screens why not go to a proper cinema then?' asked Janoo. 'However hard you try, you can't better a real cinema experience.'

'Haw, you mean to a public cinema? Like the poors?' I gasped. 'Next you'll be suggesting I take the Daewoo to Isloo or even worst, go to Jehangir's tome for a picnic like all those lower middles, Urdu medium types. I mean I don't understand . . . after all, we are also mashallah say well healed people, so why can't we also have surround sounds and other estate of the arts waali cheezain? Haan?'

'What other state-of-the-art waali cheezain did you have in mind?' asked Janoo drily.

'Well, we could have an indoor pool for a start. That way I can lie by the pool all day in my La Pearla ka swimsuit with my Prada ki dark glasses perched on the tip of my nose and a copy of *Vogue* in my paddy cured hands and a long cool glass of nimboo paani by my side like all those model types have in *Vogue*, without, thanks God, any fear of getting a tan. And also no fear of the driver and khansamah staring because the darwaza to the pool waala kamra will always be kept locked. And also if you made the pool heated then I could swim both in summers and winters, all year around. And what a good investment that would be, no?'

'Anything else?' asked Janoo.

'Well, now that you're asking, a bullet proofed car would be nice. A nice big ten ton ki Land Cruiser or if you're feeling generous then maybe even a Arrange Rover with tinted sheeshas that can't go up and down and . . .'

'But why do you need a bullet-proof car?'

'So that everyone can know how important and rich I am, baba, and sarrho and be jay of me.'

March 2013

Thousands attend Lahore Literary Festival
Butterfly enjoys the sweet peas in her garden

I told Janoo that I think so Lahore has woken up like Sleeping Beauty from a hundred years ki sleep. And Janoo said it isn't a sleep, it's a comma. Like the rest of Pakistan, Lahore has also slipped into a comma. I said but thanks God now it has woken up—just like a Bollywood heroine's sister who's had a car crash and lies for half the film with a bandage around her head totally comma dose and then suddenly her mascarad eyes flatter open and she says, 'Mein kahan hoon? Aap kaun hain?'

And he said what made me say that? To him tau Lahore still looked pretty comma dose.

And I said that haw hai, have you already forgotten that we just had a literally festival, to which not only our desi writers but also goras like Willie Dalrumple and Indians came? And there was so much of deep, deep talk and long, long discussions? And book sightings. Even I bought a book. I've forgotten its name now but it was a big one with a nice glossy cover in greens and browns. It looks so nice on my

194

coffee table next to my silver bowls, all casual, casual. I tau just love books, na.

And Lahore has also woken up because spring has come, na. My garden is full of sweet piece. I tau just love sweet piece. Vaisay tau I mainly like foreign type flowers, you know erotic ones, like orchids and tulips vaghera but for sweet piece I make an eruption to the rule. But one flower which I can't bare for one second even but which everyone else is always fainting over is a red rose. It might be cymbal of romance and love shove in America and London but I'm sorry, baba, red petals tau just remind me about graveyards and funerals and all. And Lahore airport ka arrivals floor after Hajj flight has landed.

April 2013

Election symbols assigned to political parties
Butterfly takes Janoo to a shrink

Just between you, me and the four walls, Janoo is having a nervous brake out. Not just chhota mota brake out. I mean pukka twenty-four carrot ka brake out. He won't shave, won't change out of that one crumbled shalwar kameez, won't go out—khair anti-socialist tau hamesha say tha but now he won't even take Kulchoo to play tennis or visit Lawrence Gardens for the bore walks he used to love over there. Sota bhi nahin hai. Shows no interest in food. If I say to him keh 'Chalo, Janoo, let's go to Readings, your favourite bookshop', he says, 'You go.' Talks so little that you forget he's there even. Just sits chup chaap in that armchair in our bedroom staring out at the garden as if there was a fashion show or something going on there. Aur tau aur, he won't even fight with me anymore. I can say whatever I like in front of him and he won't react. I can say Katrina Kaif is better actress than Meryl Streak, I can say George Bush and Tony Blair are my heroes, I can say cricket is most bore game ever and he won't even blink. For the hole of last month he's been like this only. I swear me and Kulchoo, we're so worried, so worried keh poocho hi na. Hundred, hundred times I've asked him keh bhai, what's the matter, tell na. But nothing. Just stares out of the window.

So finally I called up Mummy and I told her in whispers that what is happening to him. At once she said, 'Ho na ho, it is black magic. Immediately call a maulvi and get the Holy Koran read in your house and also burn red chillies and slaughter a sheep. Make sure it is black, but.' Apparently white sheeps are powerless in front of black magic. Khair, I did all that but Janoo is still same to same.

So then I called up Jonkers and first I made him swear he won't tell anyone and then I told him in whispers that what is happening to Janoo. I called Jonkers because despite of being shy and a bit of a loser socially, he is parha likha and I know he won't tell anyone. He's very pukka like that.

'From what you say,' said Jonkers, 'it sounds like he's clinically depressed. Frankly, he's been quite down over the last year or so, hasn't he? Must have tipped over into proper depression.'

'Hai, Jonky, mein kya karoon? So far tau I've hidden him in the house and I haven't let anyone get kaan-o-kaan ki khabar even, but what if people find out, haan? What if they start saying he's gone crack? His rep will be destroyed. Phir kya ho ga?'

'He hasn't gone mad. He's depressed. He needs shrinking.'

'Shrinking?' I asked. 'I should soak him in cold water and then put him outside to dry on my washing line? Like my cotton joras?'

'Not that kind of shrinking!' said Jonkers, clicking his tongue. 'He needs to find a good head doctor who can talk to him and help him get some perspective and if necessary prescribe some medication.'

'Ooh, you mean a *shrimp*? Tau then say that, na. Hai, but Jonkers, I don't want a Dr Neelum type shrimp who goes and tells everyone everything because you know, na, how much talk people do and how they take so much of delight in other people's misery? People can be so cruel, I swear.'

Jonkers was silent for so long that I thought he'd hanged up. Then he sighed and said, 'Don't worry, Apa, I won't recommend a quack. You know, don't you, that after the bombing at Data Durbar, I also hit rock bottom and if it hadn't been for Dr Hafeez, I don't know what I'd have done. He is a qualified psychiatrist and he's very good.'

'Hai, tau please Jonky darling, uss doctor ko Janoo say milva do na. Does he do house calls?'

'No. You have to go to his consulting rooms.'

'Hai, but what if anyone sees Janoo there? What if it gets out that he's seeing a shrimp?'

'We must focus on finding a cure. Not worry about what people will say.'

So anyways, Janoo is going to see this Dr Hafeez thrice a week. First time we went, me, Janoo and Jonkers, I put on my big Prada sunglasses, the ones which almost come down to my lips and draped my head in my dupatta with it half covering my face also and I sat and waited in the car, with my head bowed like a fundo's wife (in case someone saw me, na, and thought I was a patient) while Jonky took him inside. So Janoo's been going for three weeks since then and I must say it's made kaafi saara difference. He's started shaving again and showering—thanks God—and changing his clothes and two days ago he even went for a walk in Lawrence Gardens with Kulchoo. He suggested it himself only.

So yesterday Dr Hafeez called and said he wanted to speak to me alone at his office. 'Haw,' I thought, 'I hope so he won't make a pass at me.' But anyways, I went. I rapped myself in a chaddar with only my eyes showing and pretended I was a lady in purdah from a village only. And that's how I sat in the waiting room. Vaisay I was sorry to note that I recognized no one in the waiting room. I hope so this Dr Hafeez isn't just a middle class logon ka doctor, you know. I mean, I want Janoo to go to someone good and all.

I discovered two things when I went inside. One, Dr Hafeez is a seedha saadha shareef type man in his sixties and he was very proper and called me Begum Ṣahiba through out. And two, he was wearing a golden buttons waala blazer and speaking furr furr English. Which means he's a good doctor. Anyways, he told me that Janoo was making good progress but a lot depended on what sort of support structure we put in place for him at home.

'Support structure? You mean like climbing frame?' I asked from behind my chaddar. My voice was coming all muffled, muffled, so I repeated myself. 'Like jungle gym type climbing frame, you mean?'

'Er, no, I meant the help he gets from his family members.'

'Oho, that you don't need to worry about, docsaab. We

have a lot of help at home, mashallah—cook, bearer, maid, driver vaghera, vaghera.'

'I meant help as in understanding.'

'That also. Total understanding.' I wanted to tell this crack doctor that obviously the servants understand Janoo. He speaks Urdu, after all, not Russian, okay?

'Good, I'm pleased to hear that. Because I've encouraged him to involve himself once again in things that he enjoys and it would be wonderful if I could count on your support.'

'Aap fikar he na karein, docsaab. Of course you can count on me. As soon as I get home, I'll call the mazdoors and have the support structure put into place for Janoo. You think so metal would be better or wood?'

May 2013

In the run-up to elections, Tehreek-e-Taliban target secular parties
Butterfly reflects on the vagaries of fate

My kitty crowd, Mulloo, Baby, Sunny, Maha vaghera, they're all giving their votes to Imran Khan only. Except for Tara, who I think so is Ahmedi and so she doesn't want to support Imran because he's anti-Ahmedi, and Fluffy who I know is Shia and also doesn't like Imran because he never speaks against the killing of Shias. The rest, they are all obsessed with Imran's balla. Oho baba, it's his election symbol, the cricket bat, na. Nawaz's is a lion which people say looks like a billa. So balla or billa, that is the question.

'At least Imran corrupt tau nahin hai,' my kitty crowd says. 'And so what if he's stuppid? Bhai, honest tau hai na. And really, what goes of ours if he's hard on minorities and soft on Talibans, haan? It's not as if we are, God forbid, minorities or that we have to, God forbid, live with the Talibans. I mean, Lahore mein Talibans kahaan say aaye? And anyways, hotay bhi tau they're not against us Punjoos, they're against the ANP and MQM wallahs who they are killing like flies for being seculars. No baba, we tau are giving our votes to PTI, Imran's party only. By the way have you seen the new lawns? To dye for, nahin?'

Mummy and Aunty Pussy, they tau are going for Sharif's party, PML-N, because they say that Shahbaz Sharif has made Lahore look so pretty, as if it had just come out of a beauty saloon.

'Just look at all the marry golds on the Mall, darling,' Mummy said, 'and so many underpasses and flyovers and bridges and also that bus system. Not that Allah na karay one should ever have to use a bus but the poors must be so happy. And oopar say I can't stand that damn fool Imran Khan's behaviour. Threatening to beat up everyone with his bat. And calling people bad, bad names and then saying he does his best to follow the example of the Holy Prophet, may peace be upon him. Just listen to him, what a hippo crit. And beta, suna hai he wants us all to become Urdu mediums. I mean, apnay bacchay in top door English schools and our poor darling Kulchoo in a madrassah! No, ji, I'm tau for the Sharifs. At least they leave our children alone.'

Aunty Pussy, who used to be a friend of Nusrat Butto, oho baba, Benazir's mother from way back and always voted for PPP, has decided that now that Begum Bhutto bechari is no more, her vote should also be no more. So like Mummy, she's voting PML.

Janoo in the meantime, mashallah say, he's so much better. Ubhi bhi sometimes he goes all quiet but Dr Hafeez says it will take a while before he's fully himself. (I wonder whose self he is now?) Anyways, Janoo says he's caught between a rock and a hard face. He's always voted for PPP, na, because it was supposed to be leftist in the olden days. Pata hai, Bhutto even used to wear a meow cap in the '70s, that and an awami suit also. And he went and rationalized everyone's factories. And told the poors that he was going to give them all roti, kapra and makaans. So for all those reasons Janoo was his pukka fan, na (even though he wasn't a poor) and even after Bhutto was hanged he continued sporting PPP and always gave his votes to Benazir and being faithful type, even to Asif Zardari after Benazir was murdered.

But this year Janoo appears a little disheartened. He says he won't give his vote to PPP this time because they've lost the plot. (I tau thought they'd got too many plots—particularly in Bani Gala and in Isloo.) But he doesn't want to vote for Nawaz and Imran either because he says they are cowards for not speaking out against the Talibans' attacks on the secular parties. So, if you ask me, I think so he's just going to go and tear up his voting slip. Or maybe he'll vote for himself only.

And me? Sharif's lion or Imran's bat? Billa or balla? Between you, me and the four walls, neither. I tau would have voted for poor old Musharraf only. Being loyal type, I tau can't forget how he gave us Lahore Fashion Week and *Kyunke Saas Bhi Kabhi Bahu Thi* and New Year's Eve and Mobilink and all. And now look at him! One minute he's in Harry's Bar in London and next minute he's behind bars in Isloo. How funny life is, no?

Nawaz Sharif's PML-N wins a sweeping electoral victory
Butterfly goes to Sharakpur

The worst has happened. I have been brought to Sharkpur. While everyone is celebrating Nawaz's win in Lahore with big, big parties and Imran's supporters are all skulking and saying the election was drigged, I'm sitting here in bloody Sharkpur. Ji haan. Sharkpur, where people are still stuck up inside seventh century BC (Before Coffee). Hai, I could kill for a capochino.

Can you believe it? There's not a single coffee shop in the hole of this village? Zara imagine karo! Na koi coffee shop, na koi boutique, na koi beauty saloon, na spa, na mall, na cinema multiplex. I mean, one might as well be dead, no? Aur tau aur, there isn't even a proper video arcade for my poor darling Kulchoo. Not that the traitor Kulchoo seems to mind vaisay. He tau is enjoying as if he is in Swizzerland or something. All day he is striving around outside with his father in muddy khets of wheat and canes, and driving tractors, and learning to milk cows and bulls. Honestly, overnight he's become a pheasant!

So how did I land up here? Hai, it's a very sad and touchy story. You remember that bloody Dr Hafeez—baba, that brains ka doctor that Janoo was seeing when he became depress? Haan, well, he said keh Janoo must involve himself in things that he enjoys and that interest him and that his family must support him in that. Well, I was hopping against hope that Janoo will say that London interests him or that Singapore or Dubai interest him, but no, he says Sharkpur interests him. Imagine! Anyways, so when he said he wanted to go to Sharkpur for two weeks—full two weeks—Kulchoo insisted that both of us must go with him (thanks God chhuttis have happened already and we didn't have to take any holidays from school) and Jonkers said he could do with a change and he would come along also. And bus, before I knew it, I found myself back in 7 BC.

Thanks God I'd brought the last season of *Downtown Abbey* and season one and two of *Mindy Project*, my other fave TV soap at the moment. Dr Mindy Lahiri, the heroine, she's this funny Bengali lady doctor in New York and though she's fat and black she doesn't seem to know it because she's always hoping for love. Bus, so for the first three days I kept myself busy with my DVDs only. And then Janoo, Jonkers and all, they insisted I come out one day and Kulchoo said, 'Ma, you must come and see the animals.'

So, thinking we must be going to visit Janoo's cousins, I said to myself I'll show them some sophisty city style. I washed and blow dried my hair—hai, I miss Linda Chong, oho baba, my hairdresser, like astronots miss restaurants. And then I put on a pink silk ka suit with pink lace ka dupatta and pink high heeled sandals, and I also put on my pearls, and when Kulchoo came to fetch me, he looked me up and down and said, 'Going somewhere?' And I said, 'You keep quiet, ji.'

And then he put me inside the car and we drove for about five minutes past bore trees and bore fields and bore mud huts and then we drove into a sort of courtyard hummed in on four sides by mud walls and there, if you please, were about a hundred cows and sheeps and goats vaghera. I hadn't seen so many wild animals in one place since Mulloo's last dinner. 'Ta da!' said Kulchoo, throwing open his arms and pounding off to join Jonkers and Janoo who were standing by the cows. At first I thought I'd sit in the car only because no way was I going to come anywhere near this lot.

But then Janoo looked up and, catching slight of me, he gave me a big sa smile and came and helped me out of the car and, taking my hand, helped me prick my way through all the puddles and pats of pishy and potty.

'Here, look at this little fellow. He was born last week,' he said, stopping besides itna cute sa aik calf, all shaky legs and long lashes. 'Hai, shweetoo jaisa,' I said and, going up to him, I was about to pat its back when it suddenly let loose a big gush of susu, you know, small bathroom, splashing my sandals, my pink silk shalwar, everything.

'Oh my God, I'm so sorry,' said Janoo, bending down and dabbling at my sandals with his hanky. I just stood there dying to scream but couldn't in case Janoo became depress again. Kulchoo and Jonkers both had their backs to me but I could tell from the way their shoulders were shaking that they were laughing. Mir Jafars! Let them come back to Lahore and see what I do to them.

'You still look so pretty,' Janoo whispered to me. 'I'm so pleased you're here.' And just as I was about to say that chalo, it's okay, this is last season's jora in any case, we suddenly heard this loud groaning type noise and this huge sa crack looking bull with mad eyes and big curving horns, he jumped on to this cow and started raping her there and then in front of us all. And the cow, just look at her, she was least bothered. Just stood there looking around coolly as if nothing was happening. Males tau khair apnay aap ko help nahin kar saktay, that much tau we all know, but she being a woman and all, one would think she'd show some shame.

'Hai, Janoo,' I shrieked, covering Kulchoo's eyes. 'Stop them. Tell your bull to behave himself.' Janoo laughed and said, 'Relax, it's Mother Nature at work.' Dil dil mein nay socha, maybe it's in your mother's nature to behave like this but Mummy tau would rather die than have sex in public, ji.

Statistics show 'love marriages' on the rise in Pakistan
Kulchoo lectures Butterfly on feminism

Thanks God, we're all back in Lahore. Me and Janoo and Kulchoo. And thanks God Janoo is a lot, lot better. And Kulchoo Saab, well, let me tell you about him. He has got a girlfriend. Ji haan. A girlfriend, because now he's sixteen, na. And because Janoo and me, we are very liberals and modern and all, we let her come to the house. We're not like parents were in my time, you know, so strict and all that you had to meet your boyfriends chhup chhup kay by saying you're going to your friend's house and then quietly khiskoing from there on a date and then meeting in the back of a car. I tau think, bhai, kay jo kuch ho, best is apnay ghar main ho. No?

Her name is Sara and she's a little bit on the plainish side—darkish colour, smallish eyes, longish face—and not khandani from anywhere. Father has a small factory making taps and shower heads and toilet handles—I think so he does cheating of Grohe, except that his products are called Crohe. Typical do number ka maal. And mother makes furniture. You know the garage mein do tarkhaan type of business. Haan, so she has one of those. I think so it's called Woody Wood Packer.

So neither khandani nor rich from the backside. And not even pretty. Frankly speaking, baba, I am not impress. But ub what to do? Janoo says she's Kulchoo's choice and we must do respect of him and her. So I'm respecting. But on the quiet, quiet, I've had a wazifa done and I've also asked my smooth sayer, Mussarat Apa who lives in Model Town and can see into the future—she saw Imran's defeat—if this Sara is going to be, God forbid, my daughter-in-law. And she said kay no, not at all. Kulchoo will marry fair khaata peeta girl from good bagground. Like us types, you know. Inshallah. So that's why I'm quite relaxed about it and allow her aana jaana in my house.

Vaisay despite of her not so good bagground, such poocho tau she's not so bad. By that I mean that she could be worst. Says salaam properly whenever we meet. Aaj kal tau lots of girls don't even bother to notice you. And she doesn't show me moods. Always smiling in same toothy way. Has no clothes sense, unfortunately. Always in same phatti purani jeans and T-shirt and Convert kay ganday say tennis shoes. Hair is short, boy cut type. No make up, shake up, not even a slick of mascara and jewellery ka tau khair savaal hi nahi paida hota. If you'd asked me I would have said she's a gay. But Mulloo's daughter, Irum, she says lots of girls don't wear make up these days and just because you're not made up to the mines or wear six inch ki stilettoes and have bouncy Barbie type hair doesn't necessarily make you a gay. Chalo, thanks God for small messies.

She takes photos, apparently. But not nice, nice ones of models and sunsets and kites in a sunny sky and happy, healthy children carrying bunches of flowers. She takes bore ones of women in burkas crouching in corners. And black and white ones of little beggar girls with ragged hair and torn clothes and small hungry faces staring straight into the camera. You know the kind of photos I mean, na? The type that foreigners love so much of Pakistan.

Vaisay I don't know why foreigners love pictures of our poors so much. Maybe it's because when they look at us Pakistanis, all poor and starving, then they can say thanks God we are rich and healthy. And maybe these people have done something bad which is why they are looking like that and we've done something good and that's why we are looking like this. So in the end everybody gets what they deserve. They get Virgin Atlantic and David Beckham and we get PIA and Imran Khan.

I asked Kulchoo that why Sara is taking these type of photos and he said because she is a feminist. So I asked if she is feminist then why she is not more feminine, haan? And why she doesn't grow her hair long and put on lipstick and a nice chiffon sari with sequences? And he said that I didn't know anything and that I should keep my uninformed opinions to myself. And I respond karoed that is that any way to talk to your mother and he said yes, if she was going to make stupid, uneducated, ignorant statements like that. I said you are ditto your father. Badtameez and bore also. And he said I should educate myself and read a book by someone called Camilla Paagal and I said thanks but no thanks ji, and then I went and called Mussarat Apa again and she said, 'Thorha sa patients dekhain. Sub theek ho jaye ga,' and charged me five thou.

July 2013

Pakistani furniture exports rose steeply last year
Butterfly finds new respect for self-made people

Haan, so this girl Sara that I was telling you about—oho bhai, Kulchoo ki girlfriend nahin hai—the photographer, yaar, who takes bore, I mean fascinating pictures of burka waali women? Yes, her only. Well, guess what I've discovered about her? It turns out she's not so ghareeb after all. Her father's potty business—oho baba, he makes toilet handles and chilimchi kay taps vaghera—apparently it's not such a chhota sa business. In fact, it's quite a barha business. The knock-ups he makes of Grohe are so good, so good that even Grohe wallahs can't tell keh which is which. He may be a cheater cock but he's a real prince of cheater cocks. As Mummy says, whatever you do, you should it well. Anyways, he's got a huge sa show room on Brandeth Road, four floors high and all the noovo richies from Faisalabad and Gujranwala come and buy ten, ten potties and twelve, twelve tubs in one go to put inside their pink marble bathrooms with golden taps back home. So turns out Sara's daddy is, mashallah say, loaded.

And the mummy, lady owner of Woody Wood Packer, that

furniture business she runs from her garage? Uss ka bhi sun lo. Suna hai, she does so much of export that she's a businessman in her own right. Takes order peh order and sends container peh container to the Middle East, you know—to Bahrain and Saudi and Doha and Abu Dhabi and Catarrh and all. Vahaan tau suna hai they go crazy after her furniture. They love all the carving sharving with the lions' faces and the hanging ropes and the golden paint and all those big brassy nobs and knockers. They put them in their entrance and display them in their sitting room and lounge on them in their lounge.

So okay, Sara's Mummy Daddy are not khandani but at least they're khaata peeta. And that also, properly khaata peeta. They're both self mad, I'm not saying that they're not, but there's no harm in being self mad in this day and age, bhai. After all Bill Gates and J.K. Growling are also self mad millionaires, no? And nobody turns up their noses at them just because they didn't inherit their money from their Mummy Daddys and are not rich from the backside. People tau run after them to make friends with them.

Vaisay it's not like Kulchoo to ever befriend a rich person knowingly. From looking at the maskeens and yateems he's brought into this house over the years, I used to think keh maybe Kulchoo is allergic to rich people. Just look now, not one industrial typhoon's son, not a single media magnet's daughter has he ever invited over. Never has a feudal landowner or general's child been my son's friend. Only children of bechara artists and ghareeb theatre actors and small, small civil servants—grade seventeen and below—and that also in loser departments like irrigation and provincial health. Na koi customs ka officer and na koi cabinet ka secretary. Once tau he also brought home the son of a land escape gardener. I mean, if all he ever wanted to do was to become friends with a maali's child then why did we bother to send him to Aitchison College, haan? But thanks God, ub ja keh kuch hosh aye hai ussay. Maybe he's not a total crack, after all. This Sara is not bad . . . not bad at all.

So I called Mussarat Apa and I said, 'Mussarat Apa, here's another five thou, please look inside the future and tell me my son is going to stay with his girlfriend, na?'

'Aap fikar na karein,' she said. 'Jo aap chahti hain, bilkull vohi ho ga.' Honestly, what a wise person she is. So honest, so decent. And so far slighted also.

Anyways, so after dinner that night, I said to Janoo, I said, 'This girl Sara, she looks such a nice, decent, sensible type to me. And you know, she takes such interesting photos also. I'm sure she'll get a show all to herself in London soon. Foreigners tau just can't get enough of her, mashallah say. And I tau love her simple sa style. These days girls are so tacky, so over, with their false eye lashes and their pumped up lips and so much of make up and their loud designer joras. She's so different. So genuine. So I'm hoping that Sara . . .'

'Sara who?' he asked, changing the channel.

'Bhai, Kulchoo's friend. Sara Butt.'

'Unfortunate name,' he said.

'Kyoon? What's wrong with Sara Butt? Butts are not human, haan? Kya Butts feel nahin kartay?'

Kate Middleton gives birth to baby boy
Butterfly suggests names for the royal baby

Chalo, thanks God, Kate Middleclass has also made her delivery safely. (Just like Usman, our local DHL wallah who always delivers safely and also always on time.) I'm so reliefed, honestly, that she's had a boy. Not because I'm at all conservative or anything like that, taubah karo, I'm tau very modern and all, but frankly speaking, boy is still boy. However modern you get you have to admit that boy ki apni hi baat hoti hai. I shouldn't say because it's not politically erect to speak honestly, but people take you more seriously if you have sons, na.

Now take me only. People do so much izzat of me because I am mother of a son. Vaisay frankly speaking, people would do izzat of me anyways because I am khaata peeta and parha likha and from good bagground and so sophisty and well dressed and well spoken and socialist and all. I mean, what's not to respect, haan? But still, Kulchoo is the icing on top of the delicious khandani cake that I am.

Some times I think to myself that if I was a cake what sort

215

of cake would I be? Obviously I wouldn't be a pound cake or plain cake or anything bore like that. Maybe Red Velvet. Or Angel Cake. Or Double Delicious Vanilla Cupcake. I asked Janoo and he said, Fruit Cake. So I said, and you would be a Bitter Chocolate Moose.

So where was I? Haan, Kate. Mulloo and Sunny and all are saying that they don't like the name George. It's dull and bore. Kate should have named him something happening and cool like Red or Wolf or Kaz. But, baba, I totally understand Kate's choice because if I had a baby boy tomorrow, I would also name him after George Clooney. Vaisay Brad (after Brad Pitts) is also a good name. And so is Shahrukh.

I told Janoo that Kate should also have considered Shahrukh. Prince Shahrukh Windsor the Very First. Sounds so nice, no? And Janoo said that the last time he checked it wasn't common practice among members of the British royal family to name their children after Bollywood superstars.

'Kyoon ji?' I asked. 'Why is it not okay to name them after real life Bollywood heroes but completely okay to name them after fictitional Bollywood heroines? I mean, if Anne (bhai, Charles ki sarrhial bhen nahin hai?), if she can name her daughter Zara after *Veer Zara*, then why can't Kate call her son Shahrukh? Haan? Tell?' As usual he had no respond to that. And also I said, 'If Diana marhoom could name her son after a black pop star, then why you are being sick in the mud, haan?'

'I have not the faintest idea what you are going on about,' he said in a tired si voice.

'Kyoon ji, can you deny that William is named after Will. I. Am of the Black Eyed Piece, Kulchoo's most fave band?'

Anyways, I think so baby Clooney is a total shweetoo. From what I can tell from the photos, he's gone straight after his Dadi, Diana marhoom. Like her he's got blue, blue eyes and blonde say baal. (Just look at how jeans come out, hai na?) Apart from Diana he also reminded me of Kulchoo because when he was born my baby Kay also had blonde, blonde hair and light si eyes. Everyone used to say yeh tau bilkull foreigners ka baccha lagta hai. I swear I was so proud and Mummy tau dotted on him so much, so much that she kept him hidden inside a blanket for the first year of his life kay nazar na lag jaye. You know how people are jealous, na?

But then as soon as Kulchoo started running around and walking shawking, he started playing out in the sun and then bus! He got so tanned, so tanned that the tan still hasn't come off even after fifteen years. And bloody sun also burnt his blonde hair black. So unfair, I swear!

So I was saying to Kulchoo that when you apply to universities, please to apply somewhere in Scot Land or Nor Way or in north of Canada or somewhere like that where sun doesn't come out for six, six months because then maybe you'll go back to being blonde and all fair, fair. And once again everyone will die of saarh. And then they will do double respect of me because not only will I be the mother of a son but I will also be mother of a foreigner.

August 2013

The price of gold hits a record high
Butterfly welcomes her mother-in-law with open hands

The Old Bag, Janoo's mother, is here from Sharkpur (vaisay tau it's spelt Sharakpur but I prefer to call it Sharkpur, given the number of sharks who live there—The Old Bag, The Gruesome Twosome, Janoo's Ugly Sisters like in Cinderella, their loser husbands, their hideous children, millions of kameena cousins). They're all meray khoon kay pyasay and my sworn enemies. The Old Bag has brought the usual CIA spy network with her—her maid, her driver and her munshi. Ever since she turned eighty, Janoo insisted she sell her house in Lahore and move in with us.

'I really don't like the idea of her living all by herself in Lahore when she visits. I mean, the situation being what it is and she being eighty, anything could happen. It's just not safe,' he said.

'Safe for who?' I wanted to ask. 'For the poor thieves who might break in one day and be confronted by this rhino?' But being khandani and all, naturally I kept quiet.

So now she has her own sweet of rooms in our house. Janoo

insisted on it when we built our compact si 14,000 square feet ki kothi a year after we got married. At the time, I agreed because I thought Allah Mian will summon her in two, three years and she'll never get to use the rooms. So I said, 'Haan, zuroor Janoo, zuroor,' and inside I was thinking that it will make a nice guest sweet for my friends like Patty and Pinky when they visit from Karachi. But what a miscalculation, yaar. Nineteen years later, she's still as strong as a buffalo and not showing any sign of wanting to bid this world fear well.

The Old Bag's potion is called 'Bari Begum Sahiba kay kamray'. Just imagine! In the middle of my own house! But what to do; Mummy says I've got to put up with it until The Old Bag goes.

'Goes where, Mummy?' I asked her.

'Hai, beta, to meet her Maker, where else?'

After that, Mummy adviced me, it'll become Kulchoo's potion, inshallah and I'll set up my bahu there in good time, Allah willing.

Meanwhiles, thanks God, The Old Bag spends most of her time in Sharkpur and comes to Lahore only two times a year, that also at the Eids when she gives Kulchoo big fat Eidee and me usually a small piece of jewellery, and she brings lots of desi ghee and organic chickens and mangoes from the farm and desi eggs and wheat she has grown herself only on her lands. So chalo, I think, maybe if I put up with her Kulchoo's wife will keep me like a queen also.

But also I put up with The Old Bag because after all, I'm khandani and I know that one has to do respect of elders, especially those who still have lands on their name and some old khandani jewellery which they refuse to part with, claiming that they're keeping it in trust for their son's son.

'I mean, what is a sixteen year old boy going to do with forty tola solid gold karas, kundan mathapatti, rani haar and pukkay sonay ki pazaibs, not to mention the Hyderabadi guluband and the karan phool jhumkas from Multan, haan?' I asked Mummy.

'Be patient, beta,' she said, 'it'll all come to you when she goes. She's hardly going to leave it to The Gruesome Twosome.'

'How do you know?'

Mummy sighed and replied, 'Your brother's wife was eyeing my diamond bangles that I got from your Dadi and I told her she can have them when I go because they're meant to stay in the family.'

'Mummy,' I said, 'you just try giving those bangles to her and see what I do to you.'

Haw, vaisay just look at that hungry, greedy cow, my sister-in-law, eyeing her mother-in-law's jewellery like that! Honestly, what is the world coming to, haan?

September 2013

Turkish soap operas get highest TV ratings
Butterfly wonders if the Aga Khan is Turkish

I don't know about you, but I'm tau totally hooked up to these new Turkish soaps, baba. All the men in them are itnay fair jaisay and handsome also. Bhai, total Turkish Delights. Just like that Prince Rahim Aga Khan who's married that model, baba, Kendra Something. I wonder if the Aga Khans are also Turkish? I know that they live in a nice little palace near some watery type place. Was it near the Phosphorus? Or Lake Geneva? Vaisay aren't they both in Swizzerland? Or maybe the Phosphorus is a sea in Turkey only. Mother Andrews at the Convent once told me that geography wasn't my strong suit. I said, 'No, Mother, my strong suit is a green velvet jumpsuit.'

But coming back to my soaps, yesterday when Aunty Pussy called as usuals to complain about price of sabzi and how much petrol her car nuzzles, I asked her, 'Aunty, are you also hooked up to these new Turkish soaps like everyone else?'

'No, beta,' she said, 'I tau use Dove.'

Everyone's talking about this new Saudi film called *Wajda*. Apparently it's about a girl and her cycle. Everyone was saying it touches upon a taboo subject so I thought maybe it was about her monthly cycle. But no, it turns out it's about her two wheeled cycle. Apparently it's revolutionary because it's the first time ever a movie's been made by a woman director directing from a van. She shouted directions to the actors out of a loud speaker from her van. Reminded me of the Hico ice cream wallah who used to cycle past our house in summers when we were kids. He also used to shout out from a moving vehicle. 'Aaaaassss Cream.'

Apparently girls don't know how to cycle in Saudi, na. Or drive, even. Haw, I thought, someone should go and open a ladies ka driving school in Riyadh. Such a big business opportunity. Vaisay film sounds a bit bore. I mean na koi romance, na koi suspension, na koi mystery. Just a girl and her cycle. Iss say tau better is *Mein Hoon Shahid Afridi*. It's also about a boy and his bat but at least it has suspension. You know from the beginning who's going to win, but still there's suspension. Like army coos in Pakistan. You know that sooner or later they're going to happen but still there's suspension . . .

October 2013

Malala Yousafzai nominated for international awards
Flopsy and Mulloo enraged by Malala's fame

Bhai, all this Malala tamasha, it's tau made me so confused, so bemused, so defused that don't even ask. Mulloo says she's a fake and it is hundred per cent pukka that she was shot by a CIA agent. He was passing through, na, on his way from Washington to Tora Bora via Swat and he thought, 'Chalo, yeh chhota sa kaam bhi karta chaloon.' And so he shot her. So when I asked her then why have the Taliban taken credit for shooting her and also wowed to finish her off next time? Because, she said, the Taliban claimed it out of zid, na, because they're being attacked by drawns. And, she said agar drawns na hotay tau Pakistan would have been as peaceful and rich as Swizzerland. Sub Amreekans kar rahe hain.

Flopsy jo hai, she says that no, Malala's not a fake. She spoke out for girls' education and that was all fine and getting shot was also okay—and yes, she was shot by a Talib, but she's not the only one, okay—but then why did she have to go abroad for treatment? Why did she have to

223

become so attention seeking? Why did she get so much praise? Why did she give all those interviews? Why did she have to become a creation of the western media? Why did she have to bring so much shame on us? Why couldn't she have stayed in Swat only and died quietly and bravely if that was her kismet?

'But, Flopsy,' I said, 'your girls are also studying in America, one at Browns and one at BO.'

'BU,' she shouted.

'Okay, yaar, BU. You have two, two flats in Torontoe where you go every summers. You're also applying for Canadian nationalism so why are you upset at Malala going for treatment to England?'

'It's different for us, ji,' she said. 'My daughters didn't arrive on a stretcher, okay, with the world's cameras on them. They didn't ask for any attention. They didn't give any interviews to goras asking what it's like being shot in the head for going to school. They didn't ask for any films to be made on them. They didn't receive thousands of letters from school children all over the world because they told sob stories. They didn't write any books, okay? They didn't ask to be nominated for prizes and awards in the west. My daughters? They went chup chaap say on an Etihad flight, business class, thank you very much. And also, they don't stand out like Malala, in her shalwar kameez and dupatta. From the first day they ghulo milo-ed with all the other students in their tights and boots. And Seher, she has dyed her hair blonde and changed her name to Dawn and

Yasmeen is now, mashallah say, a Goth and calls herself Jasmine. My daughters are not American tools, okay?'

November 2013

NATO oil tanker torched near Khuzdar
Kulchoo breaks up with Sara Butt

Kehna nahin chahye because he's my son but honestly Kulchoo is such a loser. Straight after his father he's gone. Meri tau aik chheent bhi nahin parhi uss pay. Honestly, I'm so disappointed in him, so disappointed keh poocho hi na. What has he done? Haw, don't you know? He's spit up with his girlfriend, Sara Butt, the daughter of Woody Wood Packer and Crohe toilets wallah.

Okay, I accept that she was on the plainish side and wore old torn jeans and dirty Converts kay trainers and took bore, bore black and white photos of the poors and, okay, her parents were not khandani and she didn't have an ugla pichhla, but at least she was acchhi bhalli khaati peeti. She would have brought a kothi in her jahez and a car and maybe one or two plots even. I would have told them keh bhai, jewellery vaghera ka tau aap bother mat karein (not being khandani I don't think so they would have had nice tastes), we are not materialist types. But instead aap Sara ko bus cash day

226

dein. And living with me she would have become khandani and classy.

And apart from being khaata peeta she was nice also. She didn't show me moods and she wasn't a rude gold dogger and she wasn't a meethi chhurri either, like so many girls are nowdays. She always used to say 'salaam aunty' to me and always she was smiling her toothy smile when so many girls these days, they're so badtameez they don't even bother to look your way.

You should ask Sunny. Their son Faisal's girlfriend, she comes into the house and even if Sunny or Akbar are standing in hall way, she walks straight past them and goes straight away upstairs to his room, her heels going thik thik thik all the way up the stairs. And from there she calls on the inner com and orders the servants, 'Fata fat oopar chai lao aur French fries lao aur cheese toast lao', as if the house belonged to her from now only. Zara cheeks tau dekho! And Sunny, when she complains to Faisal, he just yawns and says, 'Chill, Ma.' As if she was a broken down fridge or something. Between you, me and the four walls, if the girl had been from a big home, I think so Sunny, would have been ready to peeyo her insults but she's not even rich, yaar. Her father, he has a chhota sa carpets ka show room on the backside of Liberty Market. I don't know from where these girls get all their hairs and braces.

But coming back to Sara, I asked Kulchoo, I said bhai, why have you spit up with her? And he said, she was very nice and they were still friends but they'd decided that for the time being they both needed their space. Aik tau children these days, they speak in such rhymes and riddles.

'Are you an astronot that you need space?' I asked him.

'You won't understand,' he said.

'Of course,' I replied, 'I'm tau aik number ki crack, na. Why should I understand anything? Acchhi bhalli larhki and you've gone and got rid off her. Anyone with half a brain sell would have hanged on to her as an investment and would have thought keh chalo, in another three, four years . . .'

'I haven't got rid of her, not that it's any of your business. We still see each other. Besides, I'm only seventeen. She's sixteen. I don't want to tie myself down to anyone. Not now, not in three, four years' time. Neither does she. Okay? Now get off my case.'

Lo, sun lo zara. This is the reward you get for paaloing them so nicely. Anyways, I became so depress that I called up Apa Mussarat, my smooth sayer, na, who can see inside the future and I told her what had happened. She told me, 'Aap loose heart na karien. Mein aap ko bata rahee hun, sub theek ho jaye ga.'

'Such?' I asked.

'Bilkull, cent per cent,' she replied.

Hai, she's so wise, Mussarat Apa, so nice.

'I'm sending your five thou ki payment with the driver just now only,' I told her.

'Ub vaisay meray rates six thousand ho gaye hain. Aap ko tau pata hai na petrol ki keemat up ho gayee tau iss vaja say meray rates bhi up ho gaye hain.'

'Acchha?' I said, wondering why her rates are tied to price

of petrol, it's not as if she's a bus driver or anything. But then I thought that maybe to travel into the future you must be needing petrol also. 'Ji ji, mein six thousand send kar rahee hun.' Thanks God for Mussarat Apa. Honestly, where would I be without her?

December 2013

**Churches given heavy police protection over Christmas
Butterfly wishes all her friends 'Marry Christmas'**

We were invited yesterday to a Christmas dinner at Sunny's. She'd cooked a turkey and made Christmas cake and plump pudding and decorated a Christmas tree—plastic ka from Dubai only. And she'd put up red and green steamers and in the bagground 'Jingle Bells' and 'Silence Knights' were playing and she'd invited the four, five Christian girls who were our classmates from the Convent with their families. But only two came because the rest have migrated to Canada and Australia because they received so many dhumkees from the fundos. The two who are left, Karen and Anita, they're also trying to migrate.

When we arrived Sunny handed out red velvet and fur ki hats just like Santa Claws wears and we played dump charades and Janoo and I, we came first and won prizes because we did a film that no one could guess. We stood with our backsides to each other, depicting an Urdu film. No one could guess, so finally we told them it was *Ass Pass*. For my prize I got a plastic key chain that said 'Mummy's Girl' and Janoo got a T-shirt that said 'I'm With Stuppid Only.' I think so it was meant for Tony, Mulloo's husband, but by mistake it came to Janoo only. Chalo, I'll ignore, being charitable sole and all.

When we came home, we discovered Kulchoo was out with his friends. So Janoo and me, we lit a log fire in the sitting room and Janoo pored himself a drink and me, I got a big mug of tea, and we sat on the sofa side by side and Janoo gazed into the fire and after a while, he said to me, 'It's been quite a year, hasn't it?'

'Hmm,' I said. 'But thanks God you are okay now, Janoo.'

'I was thinking more along the lines of elections, drones, the rise of Imran and other riveting things like that.'

'Oho, Janoo, don't be bore,' I said, prodding him in the side.

He laughed and hugged me. 'Thanks for sticking by me when I was depressed. Couldn't have been easy.'

'Haw, don't be a stuppid. Where was I going to go, haan? Anyways, you tau also put up with me, no?'

'When Kulchoo goes to college next year, it will be just you and me.'

'Yes, you and me . . . and Mummy and Jonkers and Aunty Pussy and The Old . . . I mean your mother and Mulloo and Imran Khan and Nawazu and the Talibans. You know, na, us lot only.'

Acknowledgements

My thanks, as ever, to my sister, Jugnu, who is both the source and sounding board for many of these columns and to my editor, Chiki Sarkar, for her enthusiastic yet astute reading.